THE *Asheville* CHRISTMAS WEDDING

❧ CAROLINA CHRISTMAS ✳ BOOK THREE ❧

HOPE HOLLOWAY
AND
CECELIA SCOTT

Hope Holloway and Cecelia Scott

Carolina Christmas Book 3

The Asheville Christmas Wedding

Cover design by Kim Killion, The Killion Group

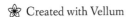 Created with Vellum

A Personal Note from the Authors

Welcome to the mountains of Asheville, North Carolina, the backdrop for our first collaborative writing endeavor. We hope you love the sisters, the story, and the setting of this holiday trilogy as much as we do. This concept was born during a week-long cabin vacation with our husbands, while we watched the sun rise over the Blue Ridge Mountains. Charmed by Asheville and the surrounding area—where Cece lived a few years ago—we started brainstorming the story of three sisters who returned to the mountains for a life-changing holiday. The idea got ahold of us and soon we were sketching out characters, plots, and a system for co-writing that has worked wonderfully. We like to think of this trilogy as a Christmas gift to our readers who've been loyal and enthusiastic since we started writing. We hope you are enchanted, delighted, and warmed by this Carolina Christmas.

With love and joy,
    Hope & Cece

This trilogy is dedicated with love to our angel in heaven, sweet Sarah.
We miss you every day.

The Carolina Christmas Series

Chapter One

Angie

ANGIE MESSINA DROPPED onto an icy wooden stair outside the cabin and stared at the piece of paper that had wrecked Christmas Day, her fortieth birthday, and possibly the rest of her life. Ignoring the cold air and wet wood, she squeezed her eyes shut and tried to *think*.

If only she could get her mind to stop spinning and her heart to stop racing, she could remember the exact words spoken to her by a stranger who'd come and gone so quickly, she swore it might have been a dream. Well, a nightmare.

What had he said?

If you don't have a physical deed to this property... then the rightful owners will take it back.

That man, a lawyer named Max Lynch, had stood in the driveway of her family's mountain property that had been theirs for one hundred years, and made the most preposterous, unthinkable, impossible claim.

This land and cabin weren't actually owned by her family.

Another family—descendants of the original landowner who had given the property to Angie's great-grandparents—had a title with their name on it and they wanted the property back...*in a week.*

Angie managed a deep breath and pushed up, shaking off the mountain chill to head inside to the large empty home. Her home now...or was it?

Before she even opened the door, she leaned back and looked up at the three stories cut from pine and built with love.

This cabin, built in the Blue Ridge Mountains just outside of Asheville, North Carolina, had a long and storied history. Her great-grandparents had built it, raised her grandmother here, and it had been a happy place of summers and Christmases for two more generations. Yes, for twenty-five years, her aunt had rented it out to vacationers, but that was because not every memory at this house was happy. Angie and her sisters had been here for Christmas the year their parents were killed in a car accident.

But they'd all worked to move beyond that memory and, for the past three and a half weeks, the Asheville cabin had been a welcoming oasis for Angie, her sisters, and their families.

But even more important, the spacious refuge had just become Angie's entire future. Moments before Max Lynch had arrived, Aunt Elizabeth, who they all thought was the rightful current owner, had handed Angie the key and told her she could live here for as long as she wanted.

With a divorce looming and her teenage daughter one hundred percent on board with a move from California to North Carolina, Angie couldn't be more grateful or thrilled. Although she'd share ownership with her two sisters, this sanctuary would give Angie and Brooke a chance to pick up the pieces of their lives and start over right here on Copper Creek Mountain.

And then some slick lawyer announced his client held the title. The only thing that trumped the title was the deed, and Angie knew that deed was not filed with the county and the lawyer said he couldn't find it, either.

So it had to be in this house. It *had* to be. All she had to do was find it and...

She turned as an engine rumbled toward the house, the sound of yet another arrival. This time, it wasn't a stranger in an expensive SUV, but the bright red truck that Uncle Sonny had just given to Angie's daughter for Christmas, back from a joy ride with the whole family.

Still standing on the deck, Angie watched the people she loved most in the world pile out of the truck, starting with her two sisters, who, along with Angie, were the Christmas-born triplets all celebrating their fortieth birthday today.

Eve climbed out first, holding hands with her husband, David, laughing at the antics of their three sons. Next was Noelle, who hoisted a little girl from the back and looked up at Jace Fleming, the single dad who'd stolen Noelle's heart and attention this month.

Aunt Elizabeth and her fiancé, Sonny McPherson, slipped out the passenger side, arm in arm as they talked about their wedding, which would take place in six days, on New Year's Eve, at Sonny's farm just down the mountain.

Last was the driver, Angie's only child and dear daughter, Brooke, who might be the most crushed by this news. With a mother's protective instinct, Angie considered sharing the news only with her sisters and Aunt Elizabeth, to save Brooke from worry.

But as quickly as she had that thought, she let it go. She and Brooke had formed a bond these past few weeks that was strong and special; she couldn't keep anything from her sixteen-year-old, including the fact that they might have to return to Northern California after all.

Brooke trotted toward the house, twirling the keys like a gunslinger. "I need to give that car a name."

"Start with calling it a truck," Aunt Elizabeth said, laughing as she put her arm around Brooke. "A 1950 Chevy, and you are a magnificent driver, my dearest darling."

"Yes!" Brooke raised a victorious fist as she beamed at Angie. "Mom, you should have come along! I nailed the..." A frown formed. "Are you okay?"

"You look pale," Elizabeth noted, coming closer with concern etched on her sixty-three-year-old features.

Eve and Noelle wore the same expression when they looked at her.

"Something happened," Angie said on a whisper, bringing all the festive laughter and chatter to a halt. "I need to talk to you. All of you."

"If Dad groveled again and you give that cheater another—"

Angie halted her daughter's words with one raised finger. "Actually, it's worse. An attorney named Max Lynch just drove up and gave me..." She lifted the paper she held in her other hand. "This. Evidently, the Delacorte family is claiming ownership of this property and the cabin. And they want us out on New Year's Day."

All of the faces around her registered total disbelief, a few even scoffing a laugh like she was kidding. After a second, it was clear that this wasn't a joke.

No one said a word for a heartbeat or two, then there was nothing but a cacophony of questions, demands, and outrage.

Angie quieted them all and led everyone to the kitchen, where the entire family gathered at the farmhouse table and long kitchen island to let her explain. Or try to.

"Okay, you probably remember that when we first got here, I found the newspaper article in the attic that informed us that this property was a gift, or at least that's what we thought," she began.

She could tell by the mix of expressions that not everyone in the room was as familiar with the details as she was.

"A couple named Louise and Keegan Winchester

gave the land to our great-grandparents, the Bensons, back in 1924," she reminded them. "Angelica Benson had risked her life to save the Winchesters' baby, named Claudia, in a small fire at Biltmore Estate, where she worked as a parlor maid."

"I remember this," James, Eve's oldest son, chimed in. "From that tour we went on."

Angie nodded, so grateful the whole family had done the Biltmore House Christmas tour. It gave them a deeper appreciation for the roles Angelica and her husband, Garland, had at the landmark mansion in Asheville. And her own work there as a volunteer had really solidified that, and maybe it could help with this problem.

"So how can they take it away?" Aunt Elizabeth asked, her blue eyes cloudy with concern. "That simply doesn't seem fair."

"No kidding," Angie agreed. "And they didn't even build the cabin. As far as I could find out from the work I've done at Biltmore House, Garland and Angelica moved out of the servants' quarters after they built this cabin sometime in the late 1920s. They moved in here, and raised their daughter, Jane, here."

"That was my mother and the triplets' grandmother," Elizabeth explained to Eve's sons, who looked confused by all the names. "And, for the record, I've paid taxes for as long as I can remember, so how can it not belong to us? Didn't you verify that when you and Brooke went to the county clerk a week or so ago?"

"Not exactly," Angie said, knowing that Aunt Elizabeth had been so consumed with Christmas, her engagement, and her upcoming wedding that she'd barely given any thought to the details of the house. But they had agreed to change the ownership from Elizabeth to her nieces, and they'd need a deed.

"That's when we first heard that there wasn't a deed on file," she explained. "The lady at the office said I could hire an attorney and do a title search, which I thought would be all we'd need. Without a deed, whoever holds the title owns the house."

"But now this lawyer shows up?" David chimed in. "And says his family holds the title? Mighty convenient timing, if you ask me. Who are these people?"

Angie nodded. "Claudia Winchester, the infant saved from the fire, grew up and married a Delacorte and had six grandchildren. The lawyer said the Delacorte family didn't even know any of this, but they were contacted by Biltmore House after I showed up and told them our connection. So this Garrett guy started digging through family paperwork and, bingo. He finds a title and decides he wants our property."

"I'm bored of this," Sawyer, Eve's youngest boy and the one with the shortest attention span, whined. "Can I go play?"

"Of course," Eve said, leaning over to give her son a kiss. "Just not alone outside."

"I'll take Tanooki!" He clutched the antique teddy bear that Eve had found in the attic and given to him for Christmas that morning.

"Be careful with that old bear," Eve said. "He's

already lost one eye and his seams are splitting. He's probably not made as well as the other ones you have."

He squeezed the toy to his chest. "I love Tanooki. I named him from *Mario Kart*," he added, as if that proved his love. "I won't lose him in the woods, Mommy."

Eve nodded, no doubt remembering that yesterday morning, they'd darn near lost Sawyer himself in those very same woods.

"I'll go with him." James, her oldest at eleven, stood, looking relieved to get away from this painfully adult gathering. "Come on, Soy Sauce. Hey, Bradley, you want to ride the snow coasters again? Cassie?"

After the four kids took off with Lucky, Sonny's golden retriever, to play, the far more serious adults all moved to gather around the table.

Aunt Elizabeth drew in a deep breath. "Angie, are you seriously telling me that we might lose this cabin?"

"Only if we can't find the deed," Angie said. "The deed—assuming our family name or our great-grandparents' names are on it—is more official and final than the title. It's that simple."

"And if we can't? Or it's not in their names?" Elizabeth asked, getting nothing but a shrug from Angie, who had no idea what to do.

"Maybe it's a matter of having a conversation with this Garrett guy," Eve suggested. "We can explain everything to him and surely he won't kick us out in a week!"

Considering the fact that he'd sent a lawyer in his

place, Angie doubted that would be an easy conversation to have.

"Well, I might meet him this week," she told them. "Remember I was asked to narrate some of the audio tour for Biltmore House? The head curator told me they had been in contact with Garrett—the only one of Claudia's grandchildren who responded to their calls—and they were attempting to get him to do part of the recording, too. They prefer descendants of the people who lived and stayed there to do the readings."

"Hopefully, by then you'll have the deed," Sonny said, putting a hand over Elizabeth's. "I sure don't want this to put a cloud over our wedding day."

"It won't," Elizabeth said, but she didn't sound very convincing.

Angie leaned closer to her. "I'll spearhead this, Aunt Elizabeth. I will not let this ruin your special day. I promise."

"Thank you, dear. But we will all help. There are a lot of nooks, crannies, and rooms in this house, and I know every one of them. I hate to tell you, though, I've never seen a deed."

"It's no doubt squirreled away somewhere," Noelle said. "We'll all help."

"We should scour the attic," Elizabeth said. "I've barely touched that in the last year that I've done renovations and that's where everything that belonged to my mother, your Granny Jane, was stored. After you girls went to college and I sold your parents' house in

Raleigh, I took a lot of the things your mother had in storage and put them up there. It might be in the mix."

"I saw some of that stuff," Angie said, remembering the day when she and Eve had gone up for the Christmas decorations. "I was surprised to find our childhood things had made their way here."

Elizabeth shrugged. "My place in New York was too small and you all were living in dorms and apartments. I never really knew what to do with things like your dad's records and personal items."

"What about when you remodeled the downstairs bedroom?" Sonny asked. "I seem to recall haulin' plenty of stuff out for trash and donations."

"Oh, dear." Elizabeth grimaced. "There was a big ol' secretary desk that I didn't want or need and I turned it over to an antique dealer. I might be able to find the receipt. What if it was in there and I didn't know it?"

Sonny put a comforting arm around her and all of them added their voices to calm her.

"Aunt Elizabeth, this isn't your fault," Angie insisted. "How would you know that no one ever filed a deed? Or that the title hadn't been changed to the Bensons' name from the original owner?"

"I just never cared about things like that," Elizabeth admitted. "My mother, your Granny Jane? She never talked about growing up here much. We didn't even come here every year until she was gone and your mother and I decided to keep the place. And the family history? I'm sorry, but I was like Sawyer—bored by it all. Your mother wasn't. And if Jackie were here..."

Eve, Noelle, and Angie all sighed in unison, sharing a look. They'd done so well this month. They'd conquered the dark past of their parents' death, and made so many new and happy memories.

They didn't want to lose that progress, or this haven, so soon after they'd rediscovered the cabin's magic.

"Our mother and father are here in spirit," Eve said.

"And maybe they'll guide us to that deed," Noelle added.

Angie's daughter leaned in close to her. "Mom," she said, "when I helped you catalog the stuff for the exhibit at Biltmore House, I read a letter from that Mrs. Winchester lady. She thanked Angelica for saving her baby and it mentioned giving the property as a gift. I don't know about stuff like that, but could that hold up in court?"

"Good thinking, Brooke," David said, pointing at his niece. "You should get a photocopy of that letter."

Angie nodded, grateful for the group brain trust. "If we had the deed, we wouldn't even have to go to court, which could take forever."

"Then let's start lookin'!" Sonny patted his legs and stood. "Divide and discover, team."

"It's Christmas Day," Angie groaned. "I know we've lost the cheer, but I hate to—"

"Darling." Elizabeth reached over the table and put

a hand on hers, tears in her eyes. "All that matters is that you and Brooke can live here. I want to keep this home in the family. You can turn it upside down, shake it hard, and take it apart beam by beam if you have to. I don't care what day it is."

"Okay, but we still have a wedding to plan," Angie reminded them.

They all shared a look that said exactly what she was thinking: if they lost the cabin, the wedding wouldn't feel very celebratory. In fact, it would be more like a funeral for the Asheville cabin that had been in their family for a hundred years.

Unless, she thought glumly, they'd just been squatters and it really belonged to another family.

"I ACTUALLY YELLED AT THE GUY." Angie looked up from the box on her lap, fading sunlight slipping through the one window in the dusty third-floor attic. "I basically pointed at him and told him to get the heck out."

"A little out of character," Eve said with a chuckle, "but a testament to how much this matters."

"As if a search of the attic on Christmas Day *and* our fortieth birthday doesn't prove it matters," Noelle said dryly, brushing some of her long dark hair off her face. "And I don't know how out of character it was," she added. "You were pretty tough on Craig when you dumped him yesterday."

Angie's eyes shuttered. "I can't believe that was yesterday. It feels like last year when I went nuclear on him in a hotel lobby."

"He deserved it," Eve chimed in. "He cheated."

"And you are a hero for dumping him," Noelle said. "I'm so dang proud of you, Ange."

Angie sighed. "I think the thing that shocks me the most is how happy Brooke is. At least, she was. Now that we might not get to live in this beautiful mountain home, I wonder if the whole 'move to Asheville' idea is going to blow up in my face."

"You have to move here!" Eve insisted. "David and I are committed to the idea now."

"And another baby?" Noelle asked. "Is that on the table?"

"It's...next to the table," Eve said, leaning back on her heels to slip her blond hair into a scrunchie she'd had on her wrist. "One massive decision at a time, I think. Once David figures out his exit strategy at his neuro-surgery group and how he can take over Dr. Robinson's family practice, we're going to put our house in Charlotte on the market and move to Hendersonville. Then we can start seriously thinking about that fourth child."

Angie groaned, lifting an envelope from the box. "Knowing all that just makes this more important. I want to be here, near you. I can't afford to buy a place here, or even rent anything decent. Oh! Could this be the deed?" She slid a card out of the envelope. "Oh, no. It's Noelle's sixth grade report card."

"Really?" Noelle leaned closer. "Did I get straight A's?"

Angie peered at the old-fashioned handwriting. "Mrs. Dombrowski said you talk too much but are very good in art class."

She snorted. "Well, I do talk a lot, and weren't my backdrops pretty last night at Cassie's Nativity play?"

They all agreed, chatting about the Christmas Eve play...and the kiss Noelle and Jace, Cassie's dad, had shared after the little girl's solo.

"Two parents couldn't have been beamed with more pride," Eve mused. "Or kissed with so much, uh, meaning."

"I just don't know what all that, uh, meaning *means*," Noelle confessed. "All I know is I'm falling hard for the guy."

"And his daughter," Eve added.

"Please." Noelle shook her head. "Cassie is the real complication. It's one thing for me to have a holiday romance with my old high school crush that begins and ends in a month while I'm visiting. But she's a seven-year-old who's never known her late mother, doesn't understand that adults can say goodbye and be cool with that. She's getting attached to me and I...I..." She dropped her head back with a grunt. "I love her more every day. What am I going to do?"

"Move here," Eve said.

"Yeah, maybe we can get a place together and stalk

the family who takes over this cabin," Angie joked, pointing to the boxes they had stopped searching to talk. "Obviously, I'm kidding, so look while you talk. And Noelle, didn't you say you had a testy conversation with your boss before the play? You haven't given us many details."

She rolled her eyes. "Most conversations are testy with Lucinda Butler, but that one was pretty bad. She wants me to come back to New York for one of Sotheby's biggest clients' New Year's Eve party."

Angie gasped. "On Aunt Elizabeth's wedding day?"

"Right? As if that's happening. I was short with her, but she's on her way to London because the guy who runs that office quit. There's drama at Sotheby's and, for once, I don't care."

"London?" Eve's eyes grew wide. "Isn't that the job you want most in the world?"

"Totally my dream, but I'm at least one year and two promotions away from even getting considered for a slot like that. I'm still not at the senior director level, but I should be. That first promotion is going to be announced—if it even happens—mid-January after the board meets. And I won't get it unless I absolutely dominate my client's estate sale, which starts the Monday after Aunt Elizabeth and Sonny get married."

Her sisters stared at her as the magnitude of her dilemma became way too clear.

"I know, I know," she said. "I'm in no position to go

falling in love with a single dad and his adorable daughter."

"Oooh. She said the L word," Angie teased.

"L?" Noelle scoffed. "L is for London, where I always thought I'd end up in a few years. I don't know. I just don't know."

"Well, I *do* know," Eve said. "I know that my family is coming here, Angie is moving here, and it only makes sense that you—"

"What's this?" Angie exclaimed, her fingers slipping over an embossed piece of parchment-type paper in an official envelope. "Feels...deed-like."

"Oh!" Noelle scooted closer, and so did Eve, abandoning her box to look over Angie's shoulder as she unfolded the paper. "What is it?"

Angie blinked at the words, her heart dropping as she read them along with her sisters.

"It's Mom and Dad's marriage certificate," Noelle whispered reverently.

"It is." Angie ran her finger over the North Carolina state seal at the top. "Jacqueline Whitaker and James Chambers."

They all let out a long, sad sigh, silent as they stared at the names of the parents they loved and missed every day.

"Hey," Eve said gently. "It's Christmas and our birthday. I don't think Mom or Dad would want us to be sad today."

"True," Noelle agreed. "But sometimes it's hard not to miss them."

"I saw two cardinals after that lawyer left," Angie told them. "All I could think of was how much Mom loved cardinals."

"And bunnies," Eve said. "Remember the two that always showed up in December and she'd leave chopped carrots in the snow and Dad would tease her?"

They chuckled at the memory, but the smiles faded as they shared another thought.

"It'll be twenty-five years this week," Noelle whispered it out loud. "Should we do something to commemorate the date?"

For a moment, no one spoke, then Eve put her hands on theirs. "Like I said, they wouldn't want us to be sad. I say we focus on the joy of the season and Aunt Elizabeth's wedding."

Noelle nodded. "You're so right, Eve. This is a week for happiness, not mourning. That's what Mom and Dad would want."

Angie slid the certificate back into the envelope. "I agree. No special ceremonies on that day, just a private hug. Unless, of course, they lead us to the deed." She put the envelope down and pointed to the boxes they'd abandoned. "Get digging so we can keep this place."

Chapter Two

Noelle

THE ATTIC SEARCH proved fruitless but the next day, they all felt a different kind of pressure. Aunt Elizabeth's wedding was five days away. They'd get married at Creekside Church, but the reception would be homespun and rustic, taking place in the massive barn on Sonny's property, Red Bridge Farm.

When Angie decided that she had to go to Biltmore House to see if they might have information on the missing deed, they all agreed that Noelle and Eve would put all their attention on the wedding. They wanted their beloved aunt's first and only wedding to be sheer perfection.

With that in mind, Noelle slid into her professional role as a project manager. With a few texts and calls, she arranged for a gathering in the great room to dole out jobs and responsibilities for the big day.

While everyone settled in, most of the talk was about the deed situation as Sonny brought his daughters up to speed.

"After a hundred years?" Caro asked, probably not

even aware that she'd already adopted the habit of putting a hand on her stomach, even though she'd only just announced her pregnancy.

"And they know nothing about this place or this mountain!" Hannah said, her dark eyes flashing with disbelief.

Jace and Cassie had come, too, which touched Noelle since they weren't officially "family." But by unspoken agreement, Jace and Noelle wanted to spend every minute together for the one week she had left in Asheville.

Even Eve's boys joined this impromptu meeting, although James and Bradley were playing handheld video games. Sawyer was on the floor, lounging next to Lucky, who flapped his tail happily by the fire.

"All right, gang," Noelle started. "Angie's gone off to Biltmore House to see if she can make any headway on our deed problem, but we have a big, beautiful project for the two people who brought us all together."

"Wedding!" Hannah raised her fist, beaming at her father. "Woo-hoo! It's happening!"

"And fast!" Elizabeth clasped her hands together, glowing with a radiance that Noelle now recognized as love. "We are officially in crunch time to make it the best day of my life. No pressure or anything." She added a playful wink, reminding Noelle of the sassy, highly accomplished woman she'd always admired, adored, and longed to emulate.

The truth was, Noelle felt all those things now, but for all different reasons. Elizabeth had found a peace that Noelle couldn't begin to describe. Was that kind of contentment even possible for Noelle? As the thought fluttered through her brain, she caught Jace looking at her, sending a now familiar thrill right down to her toes.

The man had said he'd loved her not forty-eight hours ago, and she'd yet to say those words back to him. Something was holding her back, but she wasn't quite sure—

"Who would do that, Noelle?" Caroline asked, yanking Noelle from her thoughts.

"Oh...who would..."

"String the fairy lights Aunt Elizabeth wants," Eve explained. "I'm happy to volunteer the boys, if no one falls off the hayloft."

Sawyer sat up. "I'll climb the hayloft."

"I bet you will," his mother teased, reaching down to poke the teddy bear he clutched.

"The boys are great with a task," Sonny added, giving a nod of approval to his three soon-to-be grand-nephews. "They saved my sheep."

"And I *almost* saw a bear!" Sawyer added, getting a roll of laughter from the room.

Noelle smiled. "James, Bradley, Sawyer, and Joshua"—she pointed to Caroline's little boy who'd already been embraced by Eve's sons like another brother—"you are Team Fairy Lights."

James groaned. "Can we call it something else?"

"How about the Light Brigade?" Sonny asked. "That sounds a little more manly."

"I like it," Bradley announced. "Like we're in a video game on a quest!"

The four boys all high-fived, happy with their task and the new squad name.

"Remember, I want lights everywhere," Elizabeth reminded them. "There will be six Christmas trees, both inside and in front of the barn, and multiple greenery arches in the reception area. Everything must be covered in white lights. The more the better, boys. Sonny will help you."

"We got it, Aunt Bitsy!" James gave a big thumbs-up.

"It'll be a light explosion!" Sawyer exclaimed, flinging his arms out wide.

"Wonderful." Noelle laughed softly, glancing at the list on her phone. "Next up, flowers. Eve, didn't you say you wanted to handle getting poinsettias and roses?"

"Any color will do," Elizabeth said.

"Any color?" Eve lifted a brow.

"I'm not a Bridezilla," Elizabeth joked.

"Bridezilla!" Sawyer growled in Lucky's face, making him bark and deteriorating the whole meeting with laughter.

But Noelle got it back on track, and doled out more assignments, from dealing with the caterer to finalizing the table and chair rental.

"Where will the caterer set up?" Hannah asked, frowning. "They won't cook, but they'll need a place to work."

"A caterer's tent," Noelle said. "We can get electricity out there and refrigeration."

"I'll need that for the cake," Caroline chimed in. "It's butter cream frosting and should be refrigerated, then out in the cold for an hour before serving." She made a note on her phone. "I'll handle that end of it."

Noelle happily crossed one more thing off the To Do list.

"Now, a photographer," she said.

Hannah raised her hand. "Another teacher at school does wedding photography on the weekend and I've already booked her."

"Awesome," Noelle sang.

"And I've arranged everything with the church and pastor," Sonny said. "We're all set there."

Another check mark for Noelle. "Now, what about music and dancing?"

"We've found a dance floor that we can rent, and they deliver," David said. "But they don't have any DJs available on New Year's Eve."

"I can do the music," Brooke offered. "I won't spin vinyl, but I can make an awesome playlist. I'll get everyone's requests and make sure there's lots of Boomer tunes."

That devolved into a few minutes of who was a "Boomer," but Hannah stood up and did her second-grade teacher whistle to restore order.

"Now there is the small matter of a wedding gown," Noelle said with a sly smile to her aunt. "And your bridal party. Thoughts, Aunt Elizabeth?"

"I have plenty of thoughts," she said. "The fact is, I have three nieces, and two new daughters. Not only is it way too late to get dresses, I feel like five attendants is too many for a woman my age. Plus, how could I pick one for a maid or matron of honor? All I need is one little, perfect, angelic flower girl..." She turned to Cassie and pointed a playful finger at her. "Anybody know any perfect angels who are about seven years old and can fling a few petals?"

Cassie gasped and sat up straight, her whole face bright with color. "Really, Aunt Bitsy? You want me in your wedding?"

"I do, if you would be so kind."

She let out a shriek and leaped up from her seat next to Jace, throwing her arms around Elizabeth. "Thank you! I will be the best flower girl ever!"

"I have no doubt of that, little darling." Elizabeth squeezed her.

Noelle felt the tears spring to her eyes as she watched the exchange, looking past them to Jace, who was beaming.

"I could wear my angel costume from the play," Cassie said. "It's white."

Elizabeth laughed. "I think we can get you a pretty new dress. I talked to the lady at the bridal shop in town and they have a nice selection we can buy right off the rack."

"We'll go and make it a girls' outing," Hannah said, leaning in. "And we'll all look for our dresses that day in town. Noelle is an ace personal shopper."

"Aw." Noelle placed a hand on her heart, touched. "I'm happy to be in charge of all wardrobe. What have I missed?"

"The Somethings," Elizabeth said.

"Of course." Noelle tapped her notes. "Something old, something new, something borrowed, and something blue."

Elizabeth sighed wistfully. "Is it odd that I want to be surprised?"

"Not at all!" Noelle assured her. "We got you covered." She winked at Jace, who nodded, and she put their names on the list next to "Somethings" and stepped forward and squeezed her dear aunt's hand, suddenly overcome with emotion. "You'll be a beautiful bride."

After a few minutes, they started breaking off into groups to plan their tasks and Sonny sidled up to Noelle, who'd sat down with Jace and Cassie to talk about exactly what a flower girl had to do.

"Can I chat with y'all for a moment?" he asked.

"Of course," Noelle said, sensing his tone was serious. "Have I forgotten something?"

"Oh, no, you've covered it all so beautifully," he said. "It's just that something old, new, and...borrowed surprises? I have an idea."

"Whatever you need," Jace said.

"Well, I have a locket necklace that belonged to my mother. It actually belongs to Caro now, but I think it would be nice for Bitsy to wear that day for her 'borrowed' something. The only problem is the hinge is broken and I don't know if you can get a jeweler to fix it in time. But since you're in charge of that part of the wedding, would you mind trying?"

"We'll get it fixed," Noelle assured him, touched by his sentimental side. "Is there anything else you'd like included in the 'something' collection? We still need old, new, and blue."

He chuckled. "I have nothing for old and new, but I did want to surprise her with my Lucky as the ring bearer."

Cassie gasped. "A dog in the wedding?"

Sonny's blue eyes twinkled. "Well, you know he's going to be there, so we should give him a job. And you can keep him in line, Cass."

"Yes, I can," she replied with precious seriousness.

"Maybe we can find a blue collar that holds rings," Sonny said. "I've seen those online when I was poking around."

"We'll find that," Jace assured him. "Lucky will bear the ring and the collar will be blue."

"Perfect. And for the other things, maybe you can use your judgment, Noelle. I do know she was looking at lacy gloves the other day."

"That I can handle," Noelle said. "I happen to know of some Chanel gloves she'd love. Well, the Elizabeth I *used* to know would love them."

"Chanel?" Sonny laughed. "Any Elizabeth would love those."

"No one ever rocked Chanel like Aunt Elizabeth," she agreed. "So then all we need is something old."

"What about if we use my family Bible in the ceremony?" Sonny suggested.

"Oh." Noelle touched her chest. "That would be beautiful. I'm so happy for you, Sonny."

He reached over and hugged her. "Never thought I could love again, but that Bitsy…" He shook his head. "She turned my world upside down, you know?"

Next to her, Jace exhaled. "Oh, I know." His voice was rich with meaning and Noelle knew that she had to respond to his declaration of love. She just wasn't sure when, where, or what to say.

LATER THAT AFTERNOON, Noelle and Jace dropped Cassie at Jace's parents' house for an afternoon visit. After a few minutes of chatting—more than a few, with Jace's talkative mom, Patty—they were back in his truck together and alone.

"Finally," he said, turning to her. "Just us. First time since…a while."

She smiled at him and brushed back some hair, knowing the opportunity she needed was here. "I'd love a cup of coffee."

"Copper Creek Café," he said, reaching for the ignition. "Great coffee and the best blueberry cobbler in North Carolina."

"Yes, please."

A few minutes later, they were tucked into a booth

at a cozy diner, with a hot mocha latte for her and black coffee for him, and a cobbler that could win awards on a plate between them.

Noelle took a bite and let the warm sweetness calm the jitters that came with looking into Jace's blue eyes. He gazed at her exactly as he had at the play on Christmas Eve, when he flat-out said he loved her. She'd been thrilled, dazed, and swept off her feet.

But she hadn't said the words back.

"We should make a game plan," she said, dabbing at her lips with the napkin. "For the 'somethings.'"

"I agree." He raised his brows playfully, looking at her over the top of his coffee cup. "Planning is your jam, huh? I could tell you were in your element on the wedding stuff. Bet you run a mean meeting."

She smiled. "I can lasso a few art dealers into submission."

"You sure lassoed me." He angled his head, a smile pulling at his handsome features.

She stayed quiet, thinking of all the ways to reply, dragging her stirrer through the latte foam as she thought about her life plan. She considered the upward trajectory of her career that she had spent so many years carving out, clawing her way to the top with late nights and massive deals. Her plan was to stay on top, climbing right to the summit as the VP of Luxury Art Management for Sotheby's London.

Yes, that position was a year or two away, but her career plan was on track and on time.

Then along came Jace and suddenly, her plan was...derailed.

"The plan..." she repeated slowly, lifting her gaze to meet his. "Might have...changed."

"You don't think we should start with getting the locket fixed anymore?"

Oh. *That* plan. Or was he just giving her space to bring up more personal things in her own time and way?

"I'm sure we can find a jewelry store downtown," she said, seizing the opportunity he was giving her. "Maybe they can fix that locket hinge on the spot."

He nodded. "And the other stuff?"

"Just a pair of gloves, but honestly, the gloves I want aren't going to be in Asheville." She thought for a minute. "It would cost a fortune to order them and ship in time for this weekend."

"Charlotte?" he suggested. "There are plenty of big, fancy stores there."

"That's a long drive for gloves."

He shrugged. "We'll make a day of it."

"Bring Cassie?" she asked.

"Why don't we..." He reached over the table for her hand. "Just go the two of us? Our last out-of-town date was interrupted by a filly being born."

She fought a shiver at his touch and the intensity of his voice.

"Could you handle that?" he asked when she didn't answer.

"I guess I don't know what I can handle until I'm tested."

"Do you think being with me is a test?" He sounded a little hurt.

"I think..." She didn't know how to say what she thought, mostly because she didn't fully understand it herself. But to her, love was a test—a test of faith, endurance, and the ability to handle losing it.

But she didn't want to have that conversation here and now, or maybe ever with a man who'd buried a wife he'd loved very, very much. The fact was, she had to keep this light or she'd never get on the plane, go back to her life, or be happy without him again.

It was way, way, *way* too soon to shake up everything after only dating—if you could call it that—for a few weeks.

She had to keep this surface level and fun. Nothing more.

"I think," she said with her sassiest smile, "that I have a big ol' crush on you, Jace Fleming. Same as I did when we went fishing at twelve and you kissed me at fifteen."

His eyes flickered and, almost imperceptibly, she saw him shift gears and slide from serious to playful, taking his cue from her.

It wasn't "I love you" but he probably knew it was the best he was going to get for the moment.

"You do, huh?" He gave her hand a light squeeze. "Same, Noelle Chambers. A big, bad crush and you know what we should do one of these days?"

"Winter fishing?" she guessed.

"He pointed at her. "Yes!"

"And let's definitely bring Cassie to that," she said.

"Only if you're ready to be out-fished by a seven-year-old," he said. "That kid was born with a pole in one hand and bait in the other."

She laughed, an unnatural relief washing over her as they flirted and laughed. This was better. This was easier. This was safer and so, so familiar.

This was not really what she wanted but it was the only place she'd ever gone with any man—safe behind a high and protective wall where her heart would never break again.

Chapter Three

Eve

FROM THE MOMENT Eve left for Hendersonville with David that afternoon, she was in a good mood. The drive wasn't too long, even with the day-after-Christmas traffic. And on the way down, a warm winter sun gave the whole world a glow of new possibilities.

David seemed happy and at peace, too, and the closer they got to Hendersonville, the tighter they held each other's hand.

"You're sure, aren't you?" she asked.

He tipped his head. "Nothing is certain in life, Evie."

"Spoken like a brain surgeon who's seen everything."

Nodding, he blew out a breath. "Soon to be a *former* brain surgeon and what I've seen is not enough of my family. So, from that regard, I'm sure that this is a wise decision that will benefit you and the boys, which is all I really care about. That's never been clearer to me than this month."

Eve sighed contentedly, watching the highway signs for their exit. "That cabin really is magic," she mused, then winced. "Which is why we can't lose it."

"I have to believe we can scare up the deed. Or a lawyer who can fight this."

"But if it comes to that, we'll be long evicted." She shook her head. "I'm not going to focus on that now. I'm just opening my eyes and heart to all the possibilities in Hendersonville."

"Honey, you are the happiest I can remember in years," he said, giving her hand a squeeze.

"I've been happy since the day we got married, David," she assured him. "I'm excited about the future, but I've never not been happy with you."

"It's just that I hear something in your voice that I love," he said. "So you must be certain, too."

"About you changing your job, taking over Terrance Robinson's private family practice, and moving to a small town half an hour from my aunt and possibly my sister? Maybe both sisters, if Noelle comes to her senses and lets herself fall for Jace? Yeah." She nearly vibrated at the very idea of all that wonderful stuff happening. "Color me certain."

"I mean about having another baby."

She exhaled softly, knowing that element of their lives was a big part of his decision. Yes, he promised he'd move and change jobs with "no strings attached" and she trusted him.

The fact was, David really wanted a fourth child,

and she did, too, but the weight—literally and figuratively—of that fell heavily on her shoulders.

"I'm certain I want to think about it, and I am, all the time," she said, wanting to be as totally honest with him as he'd always been with her. "Oh, look. Next exit Hendersonville."

"Where's the but?" he asked, easing the car into the far right lane.

"But...I turned forty yesterday."

"A young, healthy, vibrant forty. Also, hot." He winked.

"Thank you for all the adjectives, but forty is forty. Who knows how easily I could get pregnant?"

"We've never had an issue in the past."

"Almost seven years have passed since I conceived, David. And Sawyer was easy to make but not a breeze to carry."

"That's 'cause he's Sawyer, a ball of trouble."

She smiled as they took the exit, slowing at the bottom of the ramp to look around at the outskirts of the small town. Down here, half an hour south of Asheville, all she could see were rolling hills, sweet country stores, and precious animal and crop farms.

All of it was welcoming and warm, and only got more charming with each passing mile closer to town. Along a two-lane road, she peered between pine trees at various housing developments, some brand new, others built twenty-five years ago, but all of them well-kept and inviting.

Eve leaned her head against the window and compared some of the brick homes and adorable farmhouses to the massive Georgian they'd built outside of Charlotte. A gorgeous home, no question, and they'd spared no expense on "the house that brain surgery built."

But did she need all that room and all those upscale finishings? Not as much as she needed her husband, especially if there would be another baby.

"There's one that's gated." David slowed the speed of the car and pointed to his left at a brick guardhouse next to a decorative iron gate, a winding residential road visible behind it.

"Oh, maybe we can look there when we start house shopping." Eve smiled. "I won't be picky. This whole area is beautiful, and it all feels very safe. I'm sure we'll find something perfect."

He lifted her hand to his lips and gave it a soft kiss. "Of course we will."

She turned to him, a lump of emotion rising in her throat as she thought once again about the massive sacrifice and career change her husband was making. "Thank you for marrying me and giving me the best imaginable life."

They held hands as he found his way to a yellow two-story building just outside of town. They pulled into a tiny lot, under a wooden sign that read *Dr. Terrance Robinson, Family Medicine.*

Once more, she looked at David, knowing he was imagining how it would feel to come in here every day, to treat old and young with simple ailments instead of slipping into scrubs and the OR.

"I'm ninety-nine percent certain," he whispered as if he read her mind. "But I'll get to one hundred after this meeting with Terrance. We've talked big picture, but today is going to be nitty-gritty when, where, and how. Will you join me?"

"Why don't you talk to him alone for a while, doctor-to-doctor, and finalize the details. Once that's been done, I'll come into the meeting."

He leaned over the console and kissed her. "Ninety-nine *point five*."

Eve was still smiling as they walked into the waiting room, which was small, but clean. The furniture could use an update, and the wallpaper was past its prime, but the receptionist greeted them with a warm smile, knowing exactly who they were.

Although she offered them both a chance to go back to Dr. Robinson's office, Eve opted to stay in the waiting room, wanting to get the vibe of the kind of patients who came through.

With a quick kiss, David left and Eve settled onto a chair across from a young woman thumbing through a magazine. When she shifted in her seat and closed the magazine, setting it on the table, Eve noticed she was pregnant, with a large belly protruding from an otherwise slender figure.

The woman, who couldn't be very far into her twenties, if that, sighed and brushed away a lock of caramel-colored hair, dropping her head back as if she could fall sound asleep right there in the chair. Then she forced her head straight and blinked, running a hand over her belly and accidentally meeting Eve's gaze.

"Makes you tired, doesn't it?" Eve said with a smile.

"Next level," she agreed.

"How far along are you?"

"I'm, uh, thirty-nine weeks. Due date is January 2nd."

"Really?" Eve got a sudden burst of chills. "How exciting. Are you ready?"

She snorted. "To get her out? There are no words. For life after having a baby?" She angled her head and shuttered her blue eyes. "Not...exactly."

Eve smiled, a cascade of memories washing over her. "I know that last week is tough. All you do is stand in the nursery, look at the crib, and *imagine*. I have three boys."

"Ah." She nodded. "That's...a lot."

And yet here she was, thinking about another. "So, you're having a girl. Have you picked a name?"

The other woman searched Eve's face for a second, her expression distrustful. "I'm...kicking around...oh..." She laughed and patted her belly. "Speaking of kicking."

"Oh!" Eve had to fight the urge to leap out of her seat and feel the baby kick. "I used to love that."

She smiled and nodded, darting her gaze away as if she wanted to end the conversation. But something tapped at Eve's heart—maybe it was the low-key fear she sensed from this new mother. It was a terrifying prospect, and this girl looked so young.

"So, you almost had her on Christmas, if you're due this week," Eve said, keeping the conversation going anyway. "I was a Christmas baby. A triplet."

That got the usual raised eyebrows. "Whoa. That must have freaked your mother out."

Eve laughed. "She handled it. We all do, you know. You're probably better equipped than you realize."

Her eyes flickered with doubt. "I'm glad I didn't have it yesterday, because a Christmas Day in labor and delivery is not what Dr. Robinson signed up for when he agreed to be my doctor."

Eve frowned, not quite sure she followed that, and then realized it meant...Terrance Robinson did obstetrics? Would David be expected to do OB/GYN?

"I thought this was a family practice," Eve said. "Is there an obstetrics division here?"

She shook her head, the first hint of a smile. "Just the world's greatest doctor," she said. "Dr. R was a regular at the diner where I work. Well, worked. I started my maternity leave so I'm not serving food when my water breaks."

Eve smiled. "It can happen at the most inconvenient times."

Once again, the other woman searched Eve's face, but now that low-key suspicion seemed to transition to interest or curiosity. That made sense, since new mothers were always looking for guidance and experience.

Eve leaned forward and offered her hand. "I'm Eve Gallagher."

"Oh, hi." It was a little harder for her to bend closer, making her laugh, letting Eve see that the woman had a pretty smile that softened her otherwise chiseled features. "Gabby Colson. And, no, this place doesn't normally do babies, but Dr. R took pity on me. I've been serving him coffee and a pastry every morning for a while, and we got to talking when I was pretty early on. I asked him what I should do, since I don't have very good insurance, and he said he'd be my doctor, as long as nothing went wrong. So far, it's been easy." She laughed again. "Well, not easy, but no complications."

"That's good," Eve said, chalking up big points for Terrance Robinson. Would David be as kind and generous to a young, under-insured waitress? She'd really like to think so. "Will he deliver the baby?"

"He can, and there will be an OB/GYN on call when I go into labor." She winced. "Not looking forward to that."

"It's not so bad," Eve said, knowing full well that labor was *very* bad but that was the last thing she should tell a woman who was thirty-nine weeks pregnant. "You're young and healthy."

Gabby smiled and rubbed her belly again. "I've tried to be healthy. Watched every bite I put in my mouth, haven't had a sip of alcohol, and I gave up my once-a-week sushi fix."

"Good for you," Eve said, remembering how very

careful she'd been. And how she'd given up lots of things, including over-the-counter meds she invariably needed to take when one of the boys shared a cold. "And I hope your baby's father is willing to give you nightly foot rubs. I must have asked my husband for a hundred."

Her smile faded. "No husband, no foot rubs," she said, turning slightly as if the magazine next to her was suddenly more interesting than Eve.

The idea of going through a pregnancy alone gave Eve a punch of pain. "Oh. I'm sure that's...a challenge."

Gabby shrugged. "It is what it is."

But who was helping her? "Is your mom nearby?" Eve asked.

"No, she's, uh, actually...I don't know where she is," she admitted on a humorless smile. "Last time I saw her, I was little. My grandma mostly raised me, but she died last year."

"I'm so sorry." Eve pressed her fingers to her lips. "And your..." Her voice trailed off when Gabby shook her head with a very clear, unspoken message: no more questions. Not even a boyfriend, she surmised.

Eve studied her, fascinated by this young waitress, with no husband or mother, but resourceful enough to find a doctor and caring enough not to eat sushi.

"Well, you are one very strong young lady," Eve said softly, her voice cracking a little.

Gabby looked at her and gave a tight smile. "Strong or stupid or stubborn. I haven't quite decided yet."

"I would say strong," Eve said, touched by this

unusual mother-to-be. "Were you alone for Christmas, then?"

"Uh, yeah," Gabby said, then lifted a shoulder. "Trust me, all I did was sleep."

But where did she live? And how? And who would help her when an infant was crying in the middle of the night, and was she going back to work? And who'd watch the baby and—

"Eve?" David's voice pulled her out of her moment of maternal panic. She turned to see him standing next to the other doctor, who came closer with an extended hand, beaming at Eve.

"Good to see you again, Mrs. Gallagher." His ebony eyes were warm, and she imagined he had a lovely bedside manner and many happy patients like Gabby.

"Please, call me Eve." She shook his hand and looked from one smiling man to the other. "I take it you guys have reached an agreement?"

"Step one," Terrance said. "And step two is getting your buy-in, Eve, so I'd love to show you around." He turned and looked down at Gabby. "Give me fifteen more minutes, Gabrielle? Or are you in a rush?"

Eve's heart hitched at the kindness in his voice, and the concern. At least there was someone worried about poor Gabby and her baby girl.

"I'm cool, Dr. R." She picked up the magazine and nodded to Eve. "Do your thing and I'll be here."

With a nod of thanks, Terrance put a light hand on Eve's shoulder and ushered her toward the back. As they walked, Eve turned to get one more glimpse of the woman, who had closed her eyes and put one hand on her belly. She wanted to say something personal and encouraging, but she had no idea how to close the brief conversation.

Then David took her hand and squeezed. "I think this is a very good move, Evie," he whispered, and took her through the door into the offices.

Nearly a half hour later, after saying goodbye to Terrance and the staff they'd met, they returned to the waiting room. Gabby was gone, so she must have been called in for her appointment.

All Eve could do was say a silent prayer that the tough but tender young woman would have an easy delivery and a perfectly healthy baby.

EVE THOUGHT of Gabby again when they were sitting at a window table in Umi, a delightful Japanese restaurant that looked out at Hendersonville's Main Street. There, while munching on spring rolls and waiting for an order of sushi, Eve and David discussed Dr. Robinson's thriving practice.

Seeing the other woman in those last days of pregnancy had definitely planted a seed of uncertainty in Eve's decision about having another baby. But she didn't want to talk about that to David. There were too many other things to discuss.

"Terrance seems so excited," she said as she warmed her hands around a mug of green tea. "He really thinks you're the right doctor."

"He taught me well in med school," David said, dipping his spring roll in a sauce. "I really like his philosophy with patients, his staff, and his numbers, which were all healthy." He grinned before popping the roll into his mouth. "See what I did there?"

She laughed, enjoying the fact that David was clearly optimistic about this move. "What's the next step?" she asked.

"Obviously, I have to tie things up in Charlotte with the practice. We also will both get attorneys involved to iron out the transfer of ownership and the payments. I'm not buying the practice, but I will be assuming a few loans for equipment, nothing drastic. But there are T's to be crossed and I's to be dotted."

"How long do you think it will take?"

David considered that while he chose another roll. "Terrance is looking to turn over the practice sooner rather than later, and all I have to do back in Charlotte is oversee the initial training of a neurosurgery resident. I'm thinking this will happen in the spring, say April at the latest."

A jolt of joy skittered up Eve's spine. "When should we put the house in Charlotte on the market?"

"It'll sell fast," he said. "The other question is, when do we tell the boys."

"Sooner rather than later, don't you think? With homeschool, we can move anytime." Eve took a deep breath and exhaled slowly. "Wow, this is happening. So fast."

"When something is right, it happens fast," David said. "And with astonishing ease, I must say. It's as if this change of course was laid out for us and every door was opened for us to waltz right through at the exact perfect moment."

Eve smiled to herself, remembering Aunt Elizabeth talking about how God makes the right path so clear, you simply can't ignore it. "I'm glad you're at peace with it."

"I am," he assured her. "It's a great little practice, real small-town, family culture, and they do good work in the area. The interior could stand an update or two."

"Count on me," she said with a laugh. "We can bring in new chairs, paint, carpet, and maybe a fish tank. Don't you love that idea?"

David laughed, shaking his head as he gazed at his wife across the table with pure adoration. "Yes, but I love you even more."

As she reached over the table to take his hand, something caught her eye and she glanced outside, sucking in a breath at the sight of the pregnant Gabby waiting at the light to cross the street.

"Oh, I met that woman in the waiting room."

David turned. "She's ready to pop."

"Any day, but..." She bit her lip, watching Gabby as the light changed and she still hesitated and looked both ways before crossing to their side of the street.

"Terrance told me he's taking care of her for no

charge because her insurance is subpar and there's no doctor around who takes it," David said. "So he—"

"Hold that thought," Eve said, pushing her chair back. "I want to..." She wasn't sure what she wanted to say to the woman, but she felt like their conversation hadn't finished. And surely someone nine months pregnant and so very alone needed another woman to talk to, especially one who'd been through three pregnancies and deliveries. "Hang on a sec."

Without offering an explanation, Eve stood and hustled toward the door, opening it just as Gabby reached this side of the street, not ten feet away.

"Gabby?" Eve called.

She stopped, eyes wide in recognition. "Oh, hi."

"How did your appointment go?" Eve asked, taking a few steps closer.

Gabby looked surprised, like she didn't expect the question, or maybe she wasn't used to people truly caring. Something told Eve it was the latter.

"Good. Doc says she's dropped into place and I'm actually..." She looked left and right as if someone might be listening. "Already dilated! So maybe soon."

"It's normal to be a centimeter, even two, for up to a week," Eve said.

"Oh, really? I didn't know that. And the contractions? He said they're Braxton Hicks, but..."

"But they feel real. As long as they're not regular, you don't have to go to the hospital." *And who would be taking her?* Eve suddenly wondered. She almost asked, but it seemed like such an intrusion on her privacy.

Gabby gave a genuine smile. "Thanks, Eve. I appreciate the input."

It was all she needed to hear. "How about we get together in the next day or two?" she asked. "I'm staying with my family up in Asheville, but I can get down here easily. Can I treat you to lunch? You can ask me anything about delivery, the hospital, first baby days, anything. I'm kind of an expert and I..." She was babbling, but couldn't stop. "I want to help make it easier for you."

Gabby's shoulders sank a little as she blew out a breath. "Wow, that's so nice of you. You don't have to—"

"I'd like to," Eve said. "I know an awful lot about what you're going through and I'd love to share."

Gabby considered that for a second, then nodded. "Sure. Lunch would be great. Why don't I give you my cell number?"

"And I'll give you mine."

After they exchanged numbers, Eve pointed over her shoulder. "I'm having lunch now with my husband," she said, tempted to tell her he was taking over the practice, but knew that was too soon. "I'd ask you to join us, but...sushi."

They both laughed as if they had the smallest inside joke, and that made Eve feel inexplicably good.

"I'll text you, Gabby. Tomorrow good?"

She nodded. "Sure. I'm free unless"—she tapped the rise of her belly—"someone makes an appearance."

"I'll be in touch." With a quick goodbye, Eve

walked back into the restaurant, sliding into her seat to see David's confused look. "I made a friend," she explained. "If I'm going to live here, I'll need a few, right?"

He nodded. "Sure."

Weirdly happy, Eve folded her napkin on her lap. "Now, where were we?"

"With how much I love you."

She trilled a laugh. "Yes, more of that, if you don't mind."

Chapter Four

Angie

EVERY SINGLE TIME she walked into the grand and glorious halls of Biltmore House, Angie hummed with a sensation she couldn't describe but definitely loved. It was a marvelous mix of anticipation—what would she learn today?—and purpose and history and belonging. The cocktail of emotions had gotten familiar, but still thrilled her.

Today was no different. As she sailed past the line of tourists in front of the main entrance, greeted the tour guide who was checking tickets, and walked into George Vanderbilt's spectacular 250-room chateau, Angie couldn't help but have her spirits lifted.

She had two goals today, simple and straightforward. She wanted to talk to Marjorie Summerall, the head curator who'd been so enthused and interested in Angie's ancestors and the items she'd brought from the cabin. If the missing deed or a clue as to where it could be was somewhere in these hallowed halls or anywhere on this massive estate, Marjorie would know.

Second, she wanted to get back to the fourth-floor

servants exhibit, which would feature a replica of the room Angelica and Garland Benson lived in when they worked at Biltmore House as a married couple.

Angie had nearly completed her volunteer job of cataloging and organizing their items and wanted to finish that, as well as get her hands on the letter that Louise Winchester had written to Angelica. In her own handwriting, the late Mrs. Winchester referenced giving the Bensons property on Copper Creek Mountain.

Surely that would carry some weight with the lawyer and his client.

Since Marjorie was in a meeting behind closed doors, Angie tackled her second goal first. Up on the fourth floor, she made her way to the large laundry folding room that had been transformed into a staging area for the exhibit.

On a sigh, she dropped her coat and bag on a small bench by the door and looked over the array of personal items, clothes, letters, books, and antique furniture. Not only did she feel a bone-deep connection to the people whose lives were going to be memorialized, the actual work had become a true joy for her.

If she and Brooke lived here in Asheville, Angie would definitely seek a paid position on the Biltmore Estate. She'd study to be a curator, she'd work in the café, she'd do anything to spend her days right here.

She was so comfortable here, it was hard to believe that just a few weeks ago, she'd wandered into Biltmore House looking for answers about a newspaper article she'd found hidden in the attic. Now it felt like her second home.

Or maybe her only home, since she was about to not have one.

"Oh, here you are!" Marjorie sailed into the room, wearing her standard crisp business suit, her silver hair pulled back into a tight bun. "My assistant told me you were looking for me."

"Hello, Marjorie," Angie said, reaching out a hand to the woman who'd so quickly become a friend.

"Did you have a wonderful Christmas?" Marjorie asked with a warm smile.

"I really did." Angie smiled, too, but felt it quickly disappear. "Until I didn't."

Marjorie drew back, her blue eyes wide. "Is everything all right? Your daughter didn't leave, did she? What a lovely young lady, and so helpful when you had her here."

"Brooke's still here and neither one of us is going anywhere. But first things first," Angie said, realizing it would be rude to dive into her big problem. "How was your Christmas? Your son made it from the West Coast, baby and all?"

"Oh, yes. He and his wife and the little one showed up on Christmas Eve, along with my other son. All sorts of family fun. I loved it." She tipped her head and frowned. "What happened to steal your joy, Angie?"

Truly appreciating the other woman's concern, Angie moved her jacket to make room for Marjorie to sit down with her on the bench. "It's kind of a doozy, but you might be able to help."

"Oh, my." She took a seat and smoothed her wool skirt. "What do you need?"

Angie pressed her lips together and glanced around, zeroing in on the framed letter from Mrs. Keegan Winchester. "You remember that the Winchesters gifted property to my great-grandparents after Angelica saved their baby, Claudia."

She looked perplexed that Angie would even ask that. "Of course."

"And I told you that the Bensons built a cabin on that land, and that house is still in my family."

"You're staying there now, correct?"

She nodded. "We are until the Delacorte family kicks us out on January first and claims the land and house as its own."

The other woman gasped softly, her complexion paling a bit. "*Pardon* me?"

"The title, which the Delacorte family has in their possession, is still in the Winchester name. Garrett Delacorte, one of Claudia's grandchildren, sent a lawyer to the cabin—on Christmas Day, mind you—to announce that we were living on *their* property. Unless we can produce a deed, which carries more legal weight in North Carolina than a title does, we are essentially squatters who have to leave."

The older woman's jaw nearly hit the floor. "On Christmas Day?"

"Which is also my birthday," Angie added. "Just for more salt in the wound."

"I...I...I'm speechless!" Marjorie exclaimed. "Someone on my staff has been talking to them—to Garrett Delacorte, specifically—"

"That's the guy. He sent an attorney named Max Lynch and told us to produce a deed or get out. Please, Marjorie, tell me there's a snowball's chance that the deed is right here, right in this house, possibly left behind by Angelica and Garland."

She let out a noisy sigh. "You'd know if it was," she said.

Disappointment dropped with a thud in Angie's stomach. "Dang. I was clinging to that hope."

"You'll have to fight it in court."

"But we're going to be evicted. And..." She grimaced. "It's even worse than that. My daughter and I were planning to live there permanently."

"You're not going back to California?"

"No, I don't think I am," Angie admitted. "I'm sorry to say that my marriage is ending, and Brooke and I have decided to make a fresh start in Asheville. Needless to say, we were pretty excited about living in the cabin. But now..."

"There's no deed on file?"

Angie filled her in on the trip she'd made to the county clerk's office a while back, even before the lawyer arrived, and learned the deed was missing. "My aunt had planned to officially sign the property over to my sisters and me, so I went looking for the legal paperwork. There isn't any. I guess I would have found the Delacortes' title when I did my own title search, but with the holidays and my aunt's wedding, we didn't get that far."

"Garrett Delacorte beat you to it." She raised a suspicious eyebrow. "Interesting timing."

"The lawyer told me they had no idea they owned the property, but when the Biltmore House contacted them about this exhibit and the tie-in to Claudia, then Garrett started looking through paperwork and found the title. He hired a lawyer to take it back if we don't have a deed."

"Oh, dear." Marjorie let out an exhale. "Now I feel responsible."

"You're not. Someone in that family would have eventually found the title, I'm certain, although the whole thing's been dormant for a century."

"I will do anything to help," Marjorie assured her. "You can show him the letter and don't forget there are two newspaper articles about the event, and one confirms that the property was going to be gifted to the Bensons. I'm certain that will help the case."

"I'm not certain of anything, but I hope you're right."

"And I'll search high and low, and ask some of our filing experts if there's any chance we have anything that can help you." She reached for Angie's hand. "I want you to stay, Angie. You know I'd be thrilled to see you here every day."

Angie squeezed the other woman's hand and stood

up. "Music to my ears, Marjorie. And that just motivates me even more to find that deed."

"I'll do what I can from this end. When do you meet with the lawyer again?"

"He said to call when I found the deed."

"Take pictures of the article and letter, so you don't take the originals—"

"Of course, and thank you."

"And we'll search our archives. And don't forget, you'll be meeting Garrett Delacorte in a few days, since he agreed to do the audio recording." She grimaced. "Will that be terribly uncomfortable for you? Would you prefer I schedule the narration reading at separate times so you don't have to see him in person?"

Angie considered that, but she certainly wasn't afraid of the man. On the contrary, maybe he had a heart, and she could persuade him to back off.

"Oh, no. I'd love to see him face to face. That's going to be downtown at the corporate offices, correct?"

"Yes. I'm just waiting to hear when we'll be able to set up a studio in one of the conference rooms there."

"I'll be there, Marjorie."

"You're not losing that cabin, Angie." With another hug and some talk about the exhibit's progress, she left Angie to take careful and close pictures of the letter and newspaper articles.

After that, feeling determined, Angie dialed Max Lynch's number, praying these images would be enough to end the nightmare and get back to planning her new life in the cabin.

To her surprise, he answered the phone and agreed to meet her that afternoon in Asheville at the Green Sage Café.

Progress.

She headed there armed with optimism and photographs, hoping that would be enough to end this nightmare.

As she threaded the tables and velvet sofas of the cozy café, Angie pinned her gaze on the man who stood out among the casually dressed coffee drinkers. For one thing, he was objectively handsome. About fifty, his dark hair sprinkled with silver, with strong features and clear brown eyes, he wore that same expensive wool coat and stood when she came closer, like a gentleman.

But none of that could hide the fact that he was the devil's messenger, and to her, this tall, dark, good-looking man was nothing but a dream crusher and a fresh-start destroyer.

"Mrs. Messina." He nodded and pressed his lips together in a forced half-smile.

Angie didn't bother to smile back. "Angie is fine," she said.

"Please, have a seat." He gestured to the other chair at the two-top. "And thank you for contacting me. I hope you have the deed."

Her eyes shuttered as she sat down and looked at

him. "I have...some things, Mr. Lynch, and questions. So many questions."

"Please, call me Max, and you can ask me anything you like."

"Will it be used against me?"

He angled his head. "Let's keep everything off the record, as long as you remember I represent Mr. Delacorte and I will honor our client-attorney privilege. But I will certainly answer your questions to the best of my ability."

She nodded, inhaling slowly as the server came and took their order for coffee. When they were alone, she braced her elbows on the table and pinned her gaze on him. Maybe she should try what she hadn't when they first met—to make him see the human side of this problem. Maybe he wasn't a soulless lawyer.

"Does Garrett Delacorte really want to just boot us out of the home that's been in our family for a hundred years? One that holds countless memories and will no doubt be the site of many more?"

"Up to a year ago, the house has been a rental for twenty-five years," he said without missing a beat. "From Mr. Delacorte's perspective, it's merely passive income to your family."

She closed her eyes. "It was a rental because we couldn't bear to go there. The last Christmas we were there, when my sisters and I turned fifteen, our parents were killed in a car accident."

He winced. "I'm so sorry."

"Thank you. The memory of that kept my sisters

and me away from the cabin. It was owned—we thought—by our mother and our aunt, Elizabeth Whitaker, who has been living there for the past year, renovating." She took a breath when the server returned with coffee. "She spent a lot of money and time remodeling, and we all have come to a place of acceptance. We'd like to keep the cabin and property, and, in fact, my daughter and I are going to move in and make it our permanent home."

For a long time, he said nothing, just sipped black coffee, and looked at her. Then he cleared his throat. "I'm sorry for the inconvenience, but—"

"Inconvenience?" she shot back. "It's our *home*."

"Well, not exactly," he said. "Arguably, you haven't been there in twenty-five years. Have you?"

"No, we haven't. But that cabin—which was built by Angelica and Garland Benson, not the Winchester family—was the childhood home to my grandmother, and the summer home for my mother, aunt, and my sisters and me. It's our property."

He sighed and she saw what she hoped was a glimmer of sympathy in his dark eyes. "I'm afraid that's not what the title says. But if you find the deed, the entire thing is moot."

"I have this." She reached into her purse and pulled out her phone, clicking to the pictures she'd just taken. "This article—"

"I've seen it."

"And?"

"And it's an old newspaper article."

"That quotes Louise Winchester, your client's great-grandmother. She says, 'My heart has been saved by Mrs. Benson. Without her valor, the only thing that has ever mattered to me—my infant daughter—would surely have perished. She will be well compensated.'"

"That doesn't prove ownership."

"But the follow-up article?" Angie insisted, clicking to an image of the second yellowed newspaper she'd found in her attic. "Did you see this?"

She turned the phone to him, and he peered at the screen. She knew what he was reading, because Angie had memorized the words announcing that Louise and Keegan Winchester had gifted the Bensons with six acres of land on Copper Creek Mountain, and a substantial sum to fund the building of a home where they would live after retiring from their service at the Biltmore Estate.

"That just proves their money paid for the cabin that the Bensons were allowed to live in. Without a deed, and the title in the name of Keegan Winchester—"

"Not Garrett Delacorte," she fired back.

He tipped his head. "The Winchester family fortune has been handed down to Claudia's descendants and Mr. Delacorte has power of attorney for all his siblings and cousins."

She huffed out a breath. "So he speaks for the family who has, in your own words, a *fortune*. Plus, they didn't even know they owned this property, but now they want to take it from the family who has lived in it and cared for it for one hundred years." She tapped her hand on the table, furious. "That's preposterous."

And there it was again. The slightest glint that he had a heart and maybe, just maybe, he agreed with her.

"I understand your position, Angie, but my job is to—"

"Is this how you handle all his affairs?" she demanded. "Without empathy?"

"I'm only handling this one," he said. "He wanted a local attorney, and I do try to have empathy and fairness, but I'm afraid he has a strong case."

"Well, add this to the empathy and fairness side," she said, emotions she didn't want to feel clutching her chest. "I'm going to *move* there. With my daughter. I have to leave California where my husband is, because he cheated on me and I'm leaving him and Brooke and I were going to live there and start over and..." She muttered a curse and wiped at the tear she so did not want to shed in front of this man. "Sorry."

"Don't be," he said, real softness in his voice.

With another swipe, she looked at him, waiting for more of a reaction.

"I've been through a divorce," he said kindly. "It's hell."

Her heart shifted at the humanity in the man. "Well, so is being homeless because some rich guy found an old piece of paper and wants to add to his fortune."

For a long time, he didn't say anything, but looked

down at his coffee cup, thinking. Maybe this was it. Maybe he'd see the error of his—and his client's—ways and drop this whole stupid thing.

"If I were you, Angie, I'd find that deed."

"In other words, too bad about my divorce, my parents' passing, and my family legacy."

She saw him swallow. "My client is quite determined."

She fell against the back of the chair, pressed by defeat. "I'm going to meet your client this week."

His brows lifted. "You are?"

"We're doing the audio narration for the new exhibit featuring my great-grandparents, which has been included in the new Biltmore House tour because Angelica Benson *risked her life* and *walked into a burning room* and *saved Claudia Winchester's four-month-old life*. If she hadn't, Garrett Delacorte wouldn't be living on this Earth."

He nodded slowly, then blew out a breath. "I'm not going to be there," he said. "But I would counsel you to, um, share your feelings with Mr. Delacorte."

"Will it change his mind?"

"I don't know. You're very persuasive, Angie. And I wish you luck." With that, he put a twenty on the table and stood. "We'll be in touch."

She sat stone still as he walked out.

Chapter Five

Noelle

EVEN THOUGH CHRISTMAS Day was behind them, the town of Asheville maintained the festive holiday feel, packed with shoppers and tourists. But a seasoned New Yorker like Noelle didn't mind the crowds at all, especially with Jace and Cassie making up the perfect threesome for their errand day.

"Jewelry store first?" Jace asked after they'd parked and threaded some of the crowds on the sidewalk. "Spicer Greene is on the next block, and I think they're pretty high end."

Noelle made a funny face and looked down at Cassie. "High-end jewelry. Are there any three words a girl likes better?"

"Furry white goat," she said without a second's hesitation, making Noelle laugh heartily.

"You got me there, girl. But after a good goat, diamonds are a girl's best friend. Come on, let's get this locket fixed."

They each took one of Cassie's hands and walked side by side, looking to any outsider like a happy family of three. And to the insiders? Well, Noelle didn't hate the sensation of being connected to these two. Jace looked pretty happy, too.

And Cassie? Her tiny feet literally didn't touch the ground, but that was because Jace and Noelle frequently lifted her, gave her a swing, and enjoyed the music of her giggles.

"Oh, there's Patton Avenue Pets," Noelle said when she caught sight of the store sign. "That's where Hannah said they'll have the blue ring-holder collar. We'll go there next."

With that plan in place, they reached the jewelry store, which was crowded with customers, no doubt making returns from yesterday's Christmas gift-giving.

"Let me see if I can talk to the jeweler," Noelle said, reaching into her bag for the locket Sonny had given her. "Or make an appointment if he's busy."

"Ooh, Daddy, look at the crowns!" Cassie pointed to a case with two diamond tiaras.

"I thought you didn't care about jewelry," Jace said on a laugh.

"You keep her from buying diamonds and I'll find out about the locket." Noelle pointed at the case. "Though, as tiaras go, that'd be my favorite."

She weaved through a few people to the back table, where an older man worked quietly at a huge desk repairing jewelry.

"Any chance I can bypass the crowds and talk to you about a broken locket?" she asked.

He looked up and slid his jeweler's loupe to the

side, meeting her gaze with one that was warm and kind. "Absolutely, young lady. Let me take a look."

He pushed up and came around his table, taking the gold necklace in the palm of his weathered hand, examining the locket. "Ah, this thing is almost as old as I am," he joked.

"It's a family heirloom. And it will be, assuming you can fix it, the Something Borrowed in a wedding." Then she added, "A wedding that's happening on New Year's Eve. So, how busy are you?"

He chuckled at that and eyed her. "Your wedding? Lucky man."

"No, no. My aunt, but thank you."

With another flirtatious smile, he examined the locket, turning it over to see the initials LM on the back, reminding her that Sonny had told her this locket had been his mother's, a woman named Libby McPherson.

It hung open, revealing two small pictures, one of Sonny as a child, the other of his father.

"I assume you want to keep these pictures?"

"Oh, yes," she said. "I just need the hinge fixed."

He returned the loupe to his eye, examined the piece more closely, then nodded. "If I have a M1.6 micro screw in gold in my case at home, I can have it for you in a day or two. Let me hang on to this, get your information, and I'll let you know if I can have it by the wedding day."

She considered that. "What are the chances you will? Because if they're not good, I might have to take it somewhere else."

He looked at her, a glimmer in his eyes. "For you, gorgeous? I'll find one."

She laughed at the compliment and filled out the form to hand over the locket, then turned to look around for Cassie and Jace. She spied them in front of one of the display cabinets, deep into an inspection of whatever had caught Cassie's eye.

Furry white goats, huh? Give the kid a few years and she'd like bling as much as the next woman.

"What did you find?" she asked as she approached them.

"Your engagement ring!" Cassie exclaimed, shocking Noelle. "Look, look! The big square one with all the little diamonds around it. It's perfect for you, Miss Noelle!"

"Perfect...for..." She felt the blood rush to her cheeks as she glanced at Jace, who wore a sly smile. "Come on, you two."

"Just look at it!" Cassie insisted. "Try it on."

"No, Cassie, I can't." She glanced at the display of sparkling, jaw-dropping engagement rings. "What on Earth are you two doing over here?"

"I wanted to see them," Cassie said.

"And I..." Jace shifted from one foot to the other. "Suspect she'll like diamonds more than goats in no time."

Noelle laughed. "I was just thinking that."

Cassie grabbed her hand and pulled her closer. "Will you please try it on, Miss Noelle?"

She blinked, following Cassie's determined finger

pressed so hard that she was leaving a smudge on the glass.

"We have to go to the pet store, Cass." Noelle put a hand on her shoulder to guide her away, sucking in a soft breath when Cassie moved and revealed the whole display. The rings were so sparkly and gorgeous and designed to make a woman...*want*.

"You'll like the pet store better," Noelle said, as much to herself as to Cassie.

"Yeah, let's hit the pet store," Jace said, clearly taking pity on how uncomfortable Noelle was. "Maybe it'll be less crowded."

Cassie turned, looking confused. "Don't you ever want to get an engagement ring, Miss Noelle?"

Right that moment, she wanted all of them.

Good heavens. Who *was* she? "I've never really thought about it," she said, which was more or less the truth. Getting married had never been on Noelle's life wish list; unlike other girls, she was more interested in getting ahead than getting married.

"But the rings are so pretty!"

She gave a light laugh, unable to disagree. "There's a lot more to getting engaged, and married, than a ring, Cassie. That ring has to come with a perfect person who will love, honor, cherish, and care for you forever."

Cassie nodded. "Uh-huh. Like Daddy."

"Oh..." The word slipped out and Jace swooped in.

"Enough of this, ladies. It's time to get the Something Blue, and if we get out of *that* store without buying a kitten, we'll be lucky."

"A kitten!" Cassie practically jumped, utterly derailed from the engagement track. "Oh, can we, Daddy? Can we? It could sleep in my bed and spend the day with Sprinkles! I'll take care of it, I promise!"

Instantly, she started pulling them both to the door, a new goal in mind.

As they headed out, Jace mouthed, "Sorry about that," to Noelle.

She arched a brow. "Might have cost you a kitten."

But was that *all* it cost? Yes, they were adults who fully understood the situation from every angle. But Cassie was a child who'd probably seen a zillion happy endings in movies and thought that was how life worked. She certainly thought it was no big deal for Noelle and Jace to buy an engagement ring. How were they going to explain to Cassie that wasn't where this was going?

They needed to get on same page and tell Cassie that *this page* wasn't the one that ended with "and they lived happily ever after."

Otherwise, they were setting this child up for heartbreak and neither one of them could stand that.

To JACE's relief and Cassie's deep disappointment, there were no kittens to buy or rescue at the pet store. But she was on a kitten kick, and talked endlessly about it on the way home.

As they climbed out of the truck, Noelle held onto the only package—the perfect blue satin dog collar with two special hooks for the rings—and hoped she and Jace would have a private moment alone to talk about all that was on her mind.

"Hey, missy," he said to Cassie, giving her a playful nudge toward the small barn that doubled as a part-time animal hospital. "Chores are waiting."

"Oh, yeah! Sprinkles needs a walk." She took two steps and pivoted, pointing at them. "And a kitten to keep her company!" With that, she shot off, already singing before she got to the animals.

"Are chores waiting for me?" Noelle asked. "I can go home and get my overalls."

"You know what's waiting for you?" He put his arms around her and drew her closer, adding a light kiss to her forehead. "A fire, something warm to drink, and some time with me. How does that sound?"

She inched back and looked up at him, lost in the silvery blue of his eyes and the sheer intensity of his attention. "It sounds like you read my mind."

He walked her inside, where he kept his promise with a fire and warm tea. After Cassie came back in and got permission to take Sprinkles on a short walk, they cuddled next to each other on the living room sofa, both quiet while they let the wintry afternoon comfort them.

She decided to start first. "Jace, I think we—"

"I know, we do."

With her head still resting on his shoulder, she

smiled. "Were you as uncomfortable as I was in the jewelry store?"

"Uncomfortable?" He considered that, tugging her even closer. "That's not what I'd call it."

"How would you describe how you felt?"

He laughed softly. "I don't think you want to know that, Noelle."

"I don't?" She lifted her head and studied his profile, watching him look straight ahead at the fire. "Why not?"

"Because it wasn't what you felt."

"You don't know that," she said. "Just tell me what you felt."

"A longing," he said softly. "The likes of which I didn't ever think I could feel again."

"Oh, Jace."

"And an ache," he continued. "Like I *needed* to pick a ring, spend a fortune, and change my life."

She took a breath, closing her eyes as a wave of dizziness washed over her.

He laughed after a few seconds of silence. "I take it you felt no such longing."

"I felt...I *feel*," she corrected, "scared."

"I know, I know." He turned to face her, taking her hands. "It's scary, babe. I get that. It's a new life, a new world, and it happened fast. But Noelle, I love you. I always have, to be honest, and I don't really want to spend another twenty-five years without you."

This time, she couldn't take a breath, because it was

trapped in her chest. "I meant I was scared for Cassie," she finally managed.

"Cassie? She's going to love having you—"

She touched two fingers to his lips, silencing him. "Jace, I'm not ready for...all that. It's too much change, too much risk, too much... Just too much," she muttered, knowing she wasn't making any sense. "Change terrifies me, and I just don't make it lightly. And I don't want either one of you to get hurt. You've been through enough of that and she's just a child. How is she going to feel when I get on that plane and don't come back?"

He swallowed. "What if you...don't get on that plane?"

Silent, she leaned back, turning to look at the fire, aching for answers, formulating her thoughts, trying to make sense of something that made no sense at all: falling in love.

"Well, that's not going to happen," she finally said. "Short term? I'm very worried that Cassie is going to be brokenhearted when I leave. I don't want to be the one that drives home the lesson that people you love can't be counted on to stay."

He heaved a slow breath. "She was two and a half when Jenny died."

"And she doesn't remember loving her mother or saying goodbye," Noelle said. "But she will remember this, and me."

"She's pretty resilient," he said. "And we can drown our sorrows in chocolate milk together."

She smiled but it faded fast. "I can't stand to hurt either one of you," she whispered. "I..." She wanted to say she loved him. The words were right there, ready to come out, but something stopped her.

Because if she said them...how could she leave?

"Do you want to go back to New York that much, Noelle?"

"I don't know anymore," she confessed. "I do love it here and I can see the life but, oh, I've worked so hard for what I have. I am on the cusp of a major promotion and that is the last one I need to get in line for the job I've wanted since I started at Sotheby's—managing the London office."

He stifled a soft groan.

"I know, it seems crazy to want to live in London, but I do want that." At least, she did, before. "And London is still at least a year away, maybe two now that there's been a change in management over there. I always thought I'd get that job in my mid-forties and live there for ten years, running Sotheby's London. It's the peak of my career, and..." She glanced at him, seeing the hurt and confusion in his eyes. "I know it's just a job..."

"It's a dream, I get that," he said. "But you said London is a year or two away? What about in that time?"

"I'll be in New York."

"That's only, what, a plane ride away?"

She searched his face. "What are you suggesting?"

"Long-distance romance," he answered without

hesitation. "I'm not saying yank the rug from underneath your life or career or dreams, Noelle. I know you're getting on that plane and going home the day after Bitsy and Sonny's wedding. But does that mean, wham, we're done? Over completely?"

"I...hadn't really thought about it."

"Well, I have," he countered. "Morning, noon, and night. I know this has been fast and I know Cassie's feelings are involved, but if we talk and travel and stay connected, then I'd feel like you were giving this a fighting chance. And Cassie would get a little older and start to understand that we care for each other from...a distance."

She felt herself nod. "I guess that makes sense."

"You're not seeing anyone, and neither am I," he said, still making his case. "We can talk every day, take trips, and see where it goes. All I'm asking for is a chance, and that doesn't mean you have to change your career or promotion or life. I just want to be part of it, from here."

For a long moment, she sat very still, playing out all the scenarios in her mind. Flying down here on a regular basis, Jace visiting her and bringing Cassie. Late-night calls and surprise weekends and trips together.

"I don't know, Jace. Is long distance the perfect solution or a different road to a different heartache? And what about London? What would we do? Long distance across the ocean?"

"I guess time will tell the answers to all those questions, Noelle," he said, bringing her hand to his lips to kiss her knuckles and seal the deal. "But it beats goodbye."

"We're back!" Cassie's high-pitched voice echoed through the house. "Well, I am. Sprinkles is in the barn. I told him all about Mr. Fluffmellow."

"Who's that?" Jace asked, but Noelle laughed.

"Pretty sure that's the future kitten you don't have yet but probably will soon," she whispered.

His eyes grew wide, then soft as he laughed.

"Mr. Fluffmellow?" he called. "Don't get your heart set on that, Cassie-bug."

She came into the living room, still in her pink parka with only socks on her feet. "Hey, a girl can dream, right?" she asked, hands on hips, sass on display.

Jace launched from the sofa and lifted her in a spontaneous air spin. "Dream all you want, girl. That seems to be a thing around here."

She giggled and he glanced at Noelle, who smiled at both of them, her heart crawling up her chest and into her throat, making everything...confusing.

Chapter Six

Eve

GABBY WAS fifteen minutes late to their meeting at the funky tapas restaurant called Never Blue, prompting Eve to decide she'd been stood up. Which really shouldn't have surprised her, because the relationship was...odd. She'd probably come on too strong with the poor girl, asking questions and getting personal.

But Eve's maternal lights had been flashing and she hurt for Gabby, pregnant and alone. If she were Eve's daughter, they'd be shopping for baby clothes and making plans to—

"I'm so sorry!" Gabby darted toward the table, her wavy hair flying, a slightly grungy-looking overcoat barely covering her round belly. "I fell sound asleep!"

The confession was so real and understandable that Eve simply stood and held out her arms. "Of course you did, Mama-to-be."

Gabby gave a self-conscious laugh and returned the hug, then eased back with a hint of uncertainty in her eyes. "No one ever calls me that."

"Mama-to-be?" Eve sat back down and gestured for Gabby to do the same.

"Mama...anything." She slipped off her coat and hung it on the back of the chair before easing her body down. "And, whoa, I feel every bit of my thirty-nine weeks right now."

"I hope it wasn't too much to get you out today," Eve said.

"I was looking forward to it." Gabby let out a breath, settling in and reaching for one of the ice waters the server had poured. "Until my morning nap ran over. Is this mine?"

"Of course. And anything you want. Please, this is my treat."

She took a sip, eyeing Eve, and adjusting herself on the seat when she set the glass down.

"Hard to get comfortable, isn't it?"

She nodded with a tight smile, then leaned closer. "I guess I'm also a little uncomfortable about...this."

"Having lunch with a strange woman who befriended you in the doctor's office?" Eve asked.

Gabby laughed again, a little looser this time. "Pretty much, yeah. But, hey, I said yes because..."

Eve waited for the reason, but Gabby just took another drink and then the server came over and told them the specials. They ordered a platter of fajitas to share, chips and guac, and Gabby added a Coke, then made a funny face at Eve.

"My daily cola is my only less-than-excellent health choice. Never diet, I swear."

"I'm sure you've done everything right for your baby," she said. "And a Coke won't hurt you. I had a different weakness with each baby. With James, I craved Reuben sandwiches. With Bradley, it was the classic—ice cream with a side of anything salty, which could include a pickle. And with Sawyer?" She laughed, shaking her head. "Sugar with a side of sweets. I called him 'cupcake' and ate a few every day."

"How old are your sons?"

Eve sensed that the more Gabby knew about her, the more comfortable she'd get. She spent the next few minutes—and half a bowl of chips—telling her about the boys, their interests and personalities, and, when asked, Eve showed some pictures.

"Oh, so cute!" Gabby cooed, looking at a picture taken on Christmas Day with the boys and David. "So that was your husband who was in the waiting room yesterday? Why? Is he sick?"

"No, he's a doctor," Eve said. "And can I trust you with a major secret? He's leaving his neurosurgical group in Charlotte and taking over Dr. Robinson's family practice, right here in Hendersonville."

Gabby sucked in a soft breath, her mouth forming a perfect O of surprise.

"Oh, don't worry," Eve said, trying to interpret the reaction. "It'll take months. Terrance will be able to deliver your baby, if that's what you're concerned about."

"I'm not...no...wow."

Eve frowned, leaning in. "Wow, what?"

She just shook her head, her expression shifting from disbelief to distrust. "Is that why you're being so nice to me?" she asked. "Because I'm a patient or...what?"

"Oh, no, Gabby. I'm not..." Eve dropped back against her chair and looked across the table. "I have a maternal instinct a mile wide," she finally said. "I was the firstborn of the triplets—literally, I came on Christmas Eve when they arrived after midnight on Christmas—and I am a bit of a caretaker. And you looked like..."

"Like I needed care."

"Like you needed a friend and one who'd walked in those shoes on swollen feet before."

The younger woman smiled. "Like sausages at night," she said under her breath, making Eve laugh. "So, that's it? No other reason but you feel sorry for me?"

"I'm moving here," Eve said. "And I like making friends. And if you have a newborn when I move here, I'm happy to dole out advice from a seasoned veteran."

Gabby sighed. "Yeah, I get that," she said. "Thanks."

"No reason to thank me," Eve assured her. "And I don't feel sorry for you, but I know what it's like to be young and scared. How old are you?"

"I just turned twenty."

Wow, darn near a teenager. "I was five years younger than you when I lost both parents," Eve said as sympathy squeezed her heart. "Yes, I had my sisters and an aunt, but there's no worse feeling than being motherless."

"So, you want to be my mother?"

Eve smiled. "No, but it's interesting, isn't it? I'm forty, so in twenty years, you'll be sitting across a table looking at a twenty-year-old girl and sharing life with your daughter."

She made a small, whimpering sound, then put her hand over her lips, nothing but pain on her delicate features.

"Gabby? Are you okay?"

She nodded, swallowing hard.

"Too far into the future when you're not sure how you'll get through next week?" Eve guessed.

She nodded again. "It's not that. Well, it is. I just..." She took a moment to compose herself. "I didn't want to be a mother at twenty, Eve."

"I didn't think you planned this pregnancy."

She ran her fingers over the condensation on her water glass, thinking before she shared anything else. "When I got pregnant, Kyle, my boyfriend, really wanted me to terminate."

Eve nodded, imagining that option seemed pretty attractive to a girl this young.

"But I didn't want to," she said. "I had a lousy relationship with my mother, who just abandoned me when I was five and left me with my grandma. I wanted to be better, you know? I thought maybe me and Kyle could make it work, but he bugged out the minute I said I was keeping the baby."

Eve winced. "Just...gone? Not offering any assistance?"

"He's an artist and wants to live in a van and travel all over the country. In fact, he is doing that. And I want..." She let out a breath so long and slow, she groaned. "I want to go to college."

"Of course you do. You're a bright young woman."

"It took a few tries, but I finally got into NC State," she said, her eyes shining from a mix of unshed tears and pride.

Eve lit up. "Wow. That's fantastic, Gabby."

"It would be if child care didn't cost an arm and a leg, and if college kids wanted a roommate with a baby, and if it didn't seem like the most impossible dream ever."

At the break in Gabby's voice, Eve pressed her hands to her chest. "I know a little about impossible dreams," she whispered. "I've been reeling in them this month."

Gabby smiled, obviously confused by the comment.

"I've saved some money, and I can always waitress on any campus," she added when Eve didn't elaborate. "But, throw a baby in the mix and, whoa. That isn't easy."

And Eve was wondering how *she'd* handle another child? Her issues were nothing compared to what this girl was going through.

"So, I don't know if I'll be sitting across from her in twenty years," she said softly. "I may decide to call Child Services and put her up for adoption."

Eve sucked in a soft breath. "Really?"

"I don't have to do it right away," she said. "Like the day she's born, although that would probably be easiest. But...do you think it's a bad idea?"

"No, no. I don't think...I don't know. It's a massive decision."

"Right? That's why they said I could decide after I had her. And Dr. Robinson filled out all this paperwork for me saying how healthy I am and how I don't drink or smoke. I'm sure someone who can't have a baby would want her. And I'd want her to live in a nice house with a good family. A mom and dad. Maybe a grandma, too."

"Of course," Eve said, trying to imagine how hard that decision would be for this poor girl who had no one to even discuss it with.

"And then I could go to college," she said. "I want to study nutrition."

"Oh, that's—"

The server came with a platter of sizzling fajitas, with all the plates, fixings, and tortillas, stalling the conversation while they fussed about how good it all looked and smelled.

Eve let the difficult topic drop as they chatted about food and cooking and Gabby's interest in the science of nutrition.

Gabby lifted the small side dish full of jalapeño peppers. "I should eat these. Did you know spicy food can induce labor?"

"Or keep you up all night with heartburn," Eve countered. "Careful, Mama."

Gabby laughed, then grew serious. "Okay. Truth time. On a scale from one to ten, how bad is childbirth?"

Eleven, Eve thought, putting a hand in front of her mouth while she chewed her bite and tried to think of a less terrifying response.

"It's different for everyone. In fact, it's different for every baby."

"Were yours hard?"

"One was, one was easy, one just took his sweet time." She smiled and sipped her water. "Most important thing? Someone you love and trust to hold your hand and help you breathe."

"Dr. Robinson said the hospital will provide a doula for me if I want," she said. "Someone to do just that. Hold my hand, and remind me to breathe."

A stranger, though. Eve nodded as if that were a good solution, but she sure wished this girl had a sister or aunt or best friend in the world.

"A doula is great," Eve said. "An epidural is even greater."

That made Gabby laugh. She was completely relaxed now, asking questions and listening intently as Eve told her about all three of her experiences, from water breaking—it never did with Sawyer—to the final push.

She did her best to play down the pain and emphasize the whole maternal experience, which lasts a lifetime. But there again, she wanted to be careful. Gabby was in a precarious position and might not even keep her baby.

"Want to see the ultrasound picture?" Gabby asked after their plates had been cleared and they each had an herbal tea.

"Of course!"

"It's fairly recent, so it's a great shot of her." She fished through her bag and pulled out a small manila envelope that had clearly been placed somewhere safe and clean. She opened it carefully and pulled out a long sheet of paper with multiple images.

"Baby Colson," she said, turning the paper to Eve. "I haven't named her, because, well, if I do give her up for adoption, I don't want to force a name on someone. Plus, if I get attached to her..."

Eve's heart folded at the thought, and again at the black-and-white image. "Wow, even in six years, these things have gotten clearer. You can perfectly see her nose and eyes!"

"Isn't she pretty?"

"Breathtaking," Eve whispered, grazing one image with her finger as though she could touch the baby. "She's utterly gorgeous, Gabby."

"I know."

Eve looked up at the thick emotion in Gabby's voice, a little surprised to see a tear had fallen.

"Sometimes you love them so much it hurts," Eve said with a smile. "I feel that way every day."

Gabby nodded, fighting the tears. "I want her to

have an amazing life, you know? I just don't know if I can give that to her. And I want to have one myself, but she might keep me from getting what I want."

"Or she might be the reason you get it all."

Gabby wiped the tear, then took the ultrasound images back. "You're right. I'm just confused."

"And hormonal," Eve said. "Nothing you say or do can be held against you when you are thirty-nine weeks pregnant."

Gabby sniffled a laugh and used her napkin to dab at her tears. When she put it down, she looked across the table, all the self-conscious stiffness gone. She was warm, natural, and so incredibly young.

"Too bad you don't want to adopt her, Eve. I couldn't think of a better mother for her."

Eve just stared at her, feeling the blood drain from her head, the power-punch of shock hit her gut.

In that one sliver of time, she felt her entire world shift on its axis. In that instant, everything—*everything* —changed.

Was *that* the reason she met Gabby in the waiting room and felt so connected and concerned?

Gabby laughed and reached out her hand. "You look like you might pass out," she teased. "Here you are old enough to be my mother and I'm... Never mind. It was just a joke."

But suddenly, to Eve, it was so much more than that. It was...a possibility.

Chapter Seven

Angie

FOUR DAYS. Four lousy days.

Was it possible that was all the time Angie had left to find this deed? Yes, she reminded herself as she pulled a box of cleaning supplies down from a closet. That was exactly what she had left and...she stared at a bottle of Lysol.

The deed wasn't in this box. Or closet. Or hall.

They'd taken the attic apart, looked in every drawer in every dresser, and had moved to closets and storage areas. Uncle Sonny scoured the garage, Aunt Elizabeth turned her filing cabinet upside down and sideways, and Angie had personally dug through every nook, cranny, container, envelope, book, box, and hidey-hole that she could find.

Today, they were back at it, with Elizabeth working in the downstairs den where Noelle had been sleeping.

"This used to be a bedroom, right?" Angie asked when she came back in from checking the hall closet. She frowned as she looked around and remembered the space from childhood. Now it was an undersized den with a pullout sofa, one bookshelf that was being searched by Brooke, and a desk Noelle had been using for work. "And the room you turned into the master was an office, right?"

Elizabeth nodded. "It had the ensuite bathroom, though, and Sonny helped me add windows and a door to the deck. So lovely now. I put the pullout in here and one of the desks."

"And the other desk? Was that the roll-top style you mentioned selling to an antique store?"

She nodded. "I didn't actually sell it, but gave it on consignment."

"Oh!" Angie's eyes widened. "And they haven't contacted you to tell you it sold? Maybe they still have it. Let's call." She had her phone out in a flash. "I'll look it up. What was the name of it?" When Aunt Elizabeth didn't answer, she looked up. "You don't remember."

"Not in my wildest imagination. It was in Black Mountain, I remember that."

"Did Sonny drive it there?"

"Actually, someone from the store picked it up. I was advertising it on one of the local antique pages and they called and took it on consignment." She huffed out a breath. "I think they gave me a receipt."

"Aunt Elizabeth." Angie worked to keep the frustration out of her voice. "You're an art dealer. Surely you would keep track of furniture you give to a consignment store so you get your fair share of the sale."

"It was a piece of junk, if I may be so blunt," she said. "I don't know who bought it, but it wasn't even solid oak. I was honestly so happy someone hauled something out of here and saved Sonny the work that I forgot about it. But I really might have the receipt somewhere."

She headed to the desk that they'd already searched, pulling out the file drawer with renewed enthusiasm.

Angie's own optimism was waning, and fast. The cabin was neat and organized and they'd been through any of the places where someone might store a deed. Except for the attic and garage, which had been searched within an inch of their lives, there wasn't a lot of junk or papers.

She stood in the middle of the room, feeling a little lost, while Brooke started on the next bookshelf, flipping open books and fluttering the pages on the off-chance—so incredibly *off*—that someone had stashed the deed to the house in a decades-old book.

She glanced at the book that just hit the top of the pile—*The Catcher in the Rye*. Who'd read that one? Bending over, she picked up the hardback and opened it, seeing the light handwriting in the corner that said "Jane Benson."

"This was Granny Jane's," she said, lifting one of the crispy yellowed pages.

"She's the secret to all this," Brooke said as she shook out another book.

"What do you mean?"

"Well, she's the closest connection to Angelica and

Garland, the original owners. She lived here the longest, right?"

"Until she moved to Raleigh," Elizabeth said. "Then she met my dad, Robert, and had Jackie and me."

"But she grew up in this house," Angie said. "Did she ever talk about owning it outright? About maybe a lawyer or a survey or anything?"

Elizabeth sat upright, abandoning the file folder, her brows furrowed as she thought. "She was always weird about it."

Angie felt a tendril of worry curl around her chest. "Weird...how?"

"Just odd. Whenever the connection to Biltmore House came up, she seemed almost ashamed of it."

Angie nodded, remembering that Elizabeth had said that before. "Maybe that came from her mother, Angelica, who might have felt like the gift was too much for what she did."

"I don't know," Elizabeth said. "I barely remember Angelica. She died when I was very young, right after my grandfather. But my mother always had a thing about this cabin, like it was too rural and so far off the main road. I guess she preferred a neighborhood, like where we lived in Raleigh when Jackie and I were little."

"Maybe she knew there was no deed," Brooke said, reaching for the next book. "Maybe she knew it was only a matter of time until it got taken back by the people who gave it to them."

"Stipulations..." Angie murmured.

"What do you mean?" Elizabeth asked.

"There's a line in the letter that Louise Winchester wrote to Angelica, when she gave her a brooch. It said..." She thumbed through the photos on her phone, finding the one she'd taken of the letter when she was at Biltmore House. When she found it, she read the words out loud.

"My dearest Mrs. Benson,

"Although it has been nearly six months since we left the Biltmore Estate, I want you to know that I think about you and your bravery on a daily basis. Because you were willing to risk your own life, my baby is alive today. She's crawling, laughing, sleeping so beautifully, and I expect she'll take her first steps in a month or so. Have I thanked you enough?"

"How about a deed?" Brooke cracked. "That would thank us."

Angie smiled and kept reading. *"I know my husband gifted you with land, but that came with such stipulations and using it requires you to build a home. Is that really a gift or a monumental project? This morning, I came across this brooch that belonged to my Great-Aunt Matilda. It's always been a favorite of mine, but I want you to wear it with the knowledge that it is steeped in my appreciation and respect.*

"Someday I will tell dear Claudia that her life is a blessing, granted by a parlor maid at the Biltmore House. Her children, and her children's children, will owe you a debt of gratitude for generations to come.

"*With my deepest affection,*

"*Mrs. Keegan J. Winchester*"

For a moment, no one spoke as the weight of the letter hit them all, and not for the first time.

"So much for her children's children owing us a debt of gratitude," Elizabeth said dryly.

"What are these stipulations?" Angie asked, staring at the word. "Could we only have it for one hundred years? Did it have to do with a family living here and not renting it out? Did they have a right to take it away from us? What *stipulations*?"

"And why doesn't the word 'gift' mean anything?" Brooke whined. "They *gave* the place to us. Why take it back?"

The rise of her voice matched Angie's growing frustration and the need to do something, anything, to make progress.

"Have you scoured the internet?" Brooke asked, leaning away from the books as if she'd had enough of the task.

"Deeds aren't on the internet," Angie said. "And the lady at the county clerk's office said this one isn't even on microfiche."

"Whatever the heck that is," Brooke said. "But do I have your permission to internet-dig, Mom? If you're worried about privacy, I can go incognito so I don't leave cyber breadcrumbs when I search sites."

Angie blinked at her. "I'm not sure I have any idea what you just said, but the answer is yes. Look in every cyber nook and internet cranny if you think you can help."

"I put an envelope in a safe at Sonny's that has my birth certificate and some medical files," Elizabeth said. "Maybe the antique store receipt is there, but I doubt it."

"Maybe the deed is there!" Brooke said.

"No, he looked in it already. No deed."

Angie's heart was tired of the rollercoaster of this search. She didn't want to lose this cabin, even temporarily while they fought the battle in the courts. But it was beginning to feel like it might just go that way.

"Let's keep looking," she said, kneeling next to Brooke. "Gimme a book, honey."

She took a yellowed copy of *The Godfather* and shook it, to no avail. Like everything else on this search, she was coming up empty-handed.

THE PLANS for that night after dinner were simple: wedding centerpiece assembly. Eve had ordered all of the pieces—oversized Mason jars that needed bright silver ribbons tied around them and an array of silk flowers and feathers.

With the lack of deed-search success heavy on her heart, Angie had been looking forward to this evening all day. The boys disappeared at the first sight of flowers, begging off to play their new gaming system. David and Sonny were picking up wedding suits, and Brooke was tucked in her room having what Angie surmised was her much-needed alone time.

In the sunroom, Noelle had laid out an assembly line that apparently had to include their favorite after-dinner drink, Irish coffees, since there were four whipped cream-topped glass mugs mixed in with the decorations.

Suddenly, Noelle snapped her fingers under Angie's nose. "Earth to Angel. Earth to Angel. Come in and assemble, Angel."

Angie looked up from the sofa, realizing she sat slumped in the corner, paying zero attention to Noelle's well-thought-out centerpiece instructions. "I'm sorry," she sighed. "I'm just so worried about the deed. There's nowhere left to look."

"Sonny was so sad the receipt wasn't in my strongbox in his safe," Elizabeth said. "But I'm going to keep looking."

Keep looking. Keep looking.

Angie heard the words in her dreams now.

She forced herself to sit up straight and pay attention. "All I can think about is losing this property," she confessed. "I hate that it's put a damper on the wedding, Aunt Elizabeth."

"I'm trusting God," her aunt said, remarkably calm. "I just don't think He'd let that happen."

"Then He better drop a deed down from heaven," Angie said, trying to keep the sarcasm out of her voice.

She respected Elizabeth's faith, but faith wasn't going to save this home. A deed was.

"And that lawyer didn't give you any insights?" Noelle asked.

"Please. All I did was trauma dump on him."

"You did?" Eve asked.

"I decided that under his slick lawyerness, there had to be a man with a heart. I told him my whole story of woe—cheating husband, broken marriage, starting over at this cabin with my teenage daughter—the whole mess."

"That didn't work?" Noelle asked.

"He shared the fact that he'd had a bad divorce, too. Then told me to find the deed. My sadness had no impact on him."

"First of all," Elizabeth said, sitting closer to her, "it's not sadness or a mess. It's a whole new life, a new beginning, and hope. We live for hope!"

"I'm feeling kind of hopeless," Angie whispered. "I need something. Anything. A thread of...well, yeah, hope."

"We can't live without that," Eve said, sounding wistful enough that Angie shook off her personal blues to look hard at her sister.

"Everything okay, Eve?" she asked. "Your plan to move and for David to take over that practice still on track?"

"Rolling along nicely," she said.

"I know you've been down in Hendersonville a lot," Noelle noted. "Are you looking at houses?"

"Not really." She looked from one sister to the other. "I actually made a friend."

"Without us?" Angie teased. "Who is this interloper?"

"Just a young woman who is a patient of Dr. Robinson's. I met her in the waiting room when David was having his meeting and we kind of hit it off." She reached for her Irish coffee. "We had lunch today."

"Oh, okay." Noelle looked like she expected more, too, but let it go. "Well, the lawyer is just the go-between," she added, bringing the conversation back to Angie. "Aren't you going to meet this Garrett Delacorte guy soon? That's who needs to know your story. That's who needs to have a heart. I think you should pull yourself out of your blues and focus on that meeting. You'll fix it that day."

Oh, how she hoped Noelle was right. "He's allegedly coming to do the recording," Angie said. "Who knows? He could back out at the last minute. We know nothing about Garrett Delacorte."

"Oh, yes, we do." The singsong announcement came from Brooke, who practically danced into the sunroom.

All four of them turned to her with expectant looks.

She held up her phone and rocked it from side to side. "I did a little cyberstalking."

"Oh, boy," Angie said, falling back on the sofa. "Do we want to know?"

"Yes, you do." She plopped down in front of the centerpiece-laden coffee table, moved a Mason jar, and faced them all. "I am officially in the DMs of a certain Sam Delacorte, sixteen years old, seriously attractive, stupidly rich, and very close to his daddy, none other than Garrett himself."

And all four jaws dropped.

"What does that mean, you're in the DMs?" Elizabeth asked.

"I sent a direct message to Sammy boy, whose real name is Samson, if you can believe that."

"Oh!" Elizabeth clapped her hands. "A Biblical name. I like that."

"A rich kid's name," she said. "Which this guy is. He fits the profile to a T."

"Wait, wait." Angie held up both hands. "You contacted a Delacorte? Brooke! Do you think that's a good idea?"

"I think it's one way to find out what that family is all about," she countered. "Sending a message to a guy out of the blue isn't weird. He's cute, I'm cute, and I pinged him on Instagram. It's not a huge deal."

"We might be embroiled in a lawsuit with this family." Even as she said the words, Angie hoped they would never come true.

"It's fine, Mom. I won't say anything that can be used against us. And believe me, I can talk this kid's language. He's exactly like the idiots at Willows Academy I want to avoid."

"So you DM'd him," Noelle said dryly. "Be careful, Brooke."

"I am, Aunt Noelle." She glanced at the phone. "He hasn't even—scratch that. He just responded!"

"Oh!"

"What did he say?"

"Let's read it!"

"Is there a picture?"

Brooke started laughing, using the phone to point to all of them. "Not interested, huh?"

"Just wary," Angie corrected. "Share, girl."

"He said, 'Hey.'"

"Hey?" Elizabeth scoffed. "Can't he do better than that?"

"We're just getting started," Brooke told her. "All decent convos start with, 'Hey.'"

"Huh." Elizabeth took a sip of Irish coffee. "Not in my day."

Brooke started typing again, then paused, looking up. "Should I tell him why I reached out or not?"

"Yes," Elizabeth said.

"Maybe," Eve and Noelle chimed in.

"Absolutely not!" Angie insisted. "What if we have to face him in court?"

"What if he knows where the deed is?" Brooke countered. "What if his dad has it and is hiding it on purpose so that he can have this property?"

They gasped in unison.

"I never thought of that," Angie said, her heart sinking to the floor. "Would Garrett double-cross us like that?"

Brooke lifted a shoulder. "I think double-cross is

this guy's middle name. But we need to decide. Truth or fake-out?"

All four of them looked at each other, uncertain.

"I say be honest," Elizabeth said. "It's always the best policy."

"Oh, wait, wait," Brooke said, holding up the phone. "He already knows."

"What?" Angie asked. Brooke angled the phone so Angie could read the note. "'I recognize your name. I heard my dad say it to one of my uncles.'"

"Now what?" Brooke asked.

"Now...ask him if his dad has a heart," Eve said softly. "And ask him how much taking one family's future bothers him."

"No, no. Just develop a rapport," Noelle said. "See if you can sweettalk info out of him."

"Remind him that he wouldn't be alive today if Angelica Benson hadn't risked life, limb, and a raging fire to save his great-grandmother's life," Angie suggested.

"Yeah! Tell him that!"

"But be honest."

"And friendly."

Brooke just started laughing as she pushed up. "Ladies, I'm going to handle this like the Gen Z girl I am. On my own, over text, in my own voice. You have to trust me, and I'll be back."

Their mouths gaped again as she zoomed out, phone in hand, thumbs flying.

They commenced centerpiece assembly, but

tension stretched through the room until Brooke came bounding back in a little while later and they demanded an update.

"One, he's kind of sweet, I'm not going to lie," she started. "Two, his father is a hard...er, tough negotiator who, according to him, never met a deal he wouldn't win."

"Ouch," Angie whispered.

"And three? I'm seeing him at the recording session for Biltmore House. He said his dad invited him and he thought it would be lame but now..." She shrugged. "He wants to meet in person."

"Where does he live?" Eve asked.

"Miami." She smiled and jabbed Noelle with the phone. "Maybe I'll have a long-distance romance, too."

"Romance?" Angie squawked. "You are not getting romantic with the son of the man who wants to pillage our home and erase our family history."

Brooke laughed softly. "Dramatic much, Mom? Don't worry, I'm kidding. But he's a decent dude who might help us get some insight. I don't see a downside."

"Except his father could have been on the other end doing the whole Cyrano de Bergerac thing for him," Angie said.

"I have no idea who Cyrano de Whateverac is," Brooke said. "But, Mom, listen to me." She sat down next to Angie and put an arm around her. "I want to help. I'm going to live here, too, and I have to tell you, I'm not giving up easily."

Angie closed her eyes and leaned into Brooke,

loving her with every cell in her body and determined to give her all she deserved in life. "Okay, do your Gen Z thing, Brooke. But, for the love of God, don't marry the guy."

"Might be the only way to get our cabin back," Brooke said on a sigh.

Sadly, right that moment, she wasn't wrong.

Chapter Eight

Noelle

DRESS SHOPPING WAS the day Noelle had been most excited about. Aunt Elizabeth had made an appointment at a lovely bridal shop in town, and they had the store to themselves. Good thing, because there were five not-bridesmaids who would have opinions, one flower girl who was climbing out of her skin with excitement, and the world's most beautiful sixty-three-year-old bride.

Not five minutes after the cork in the first bottle of champagne popped and the ladies filled the velvet sofas to watch Elizabeth try on dresses, Noelle's cell vibrated with a call from her boss, straight from Sotheby's London.

Why couldn't Lucinda ever call when Noelle was at her desk? She'd worked from six this morning to eleven a.m., nearly finishing the entire estate sale project that had been thrown at her earlier this month.

She couldn't ignore the call. And with the time difference, she had to take it now.

"Don't model anything yet," she said, holding up

her phone and walking toward the front. "Quick call for me."

They groaned, but she ignored them, pulling the heavy glass door open and standing in the warm, enclosed front vestibule, grateful she didn't have to take the call on the street.

"How's London treating you, Lucinda?" she asked as she answered.

"Don't ask. Nigel left this place a hot mess with unfinished deals left and right."

"Anything I can help with?" Noelle asked without thinking, then wished she could kick herself, because the answer would, of course, be more work she didn't want this week.

"Just a simple yes or no, Noelle."

She sighed, knowing Lucinda was back on the New Year's Eve party their biggest client was having. "I'm sorry, but I cannot make Colin Van Zant's party. I'm here for my aunt's wedding and—"

"No, I've accepted that and am sending a replacement. It's fine."

Noelle bristled a little at how easily she was replaced, but forced herself to see the very bright side. She was off the hook to represent Sotheby's at their important client's night.

"I need a yes or no that you'll be in New York on the morning of January second," Lucinda said.

Noelle hated it, but she'd be there. "I will," she confirmed.

"Because the management reorg meeting is taking place that day and I want you there."

"Oh?" That was a change. "I thought the board was meeting in mid-January, and that was when they'd decide on my promotion to senior director."

Lucinda was quiet for a second, then said, "It's all been moved up."

Noelle squeezed her eyes shut and decided she had to know anything Lucinda was willing to tell her. "Do you think I'll get the promotion, Lucinda?"

"I do," she said without hesitation. "Assuming you knock the estate sale out of the park that week."

"All the way out of the park, I promise."

"Good. Then you might get my office."

"What? Where will you be?" Noelle asked.

"I might take Nigel's job and stay in London."

"Oh." Noelle leaned against the cool door and considered what that meant, long term. For one thing, it meant Noelle's job in New York would be more pleasant, since Lucinda was a tough boss. But it also meant Lucinda, who was in her early fifties with no sign of retirement, could be running the London operation for a long, long time. Maybe a decade or more, delaying Noelle's dream for many years. Without the possibility of managing the London operation in a year or two, working at Sotheby's lost some of its luster.

That would answer the "how do we do long distance in London" question that had plagued her since she and Jace had talked about it.

"Well, that would be a huge change," Noelle said, thinking more of her own change than Lucinda's.

"I like it here," the other woman said. "It's a nice change from New York and the people are smart. But all that is yet to be decided. For now, I need to know if your little field trip to the mountains will end for real and for good when we flip the calendar to a new year. If I'm in London, I'll need you to step it up like never before."

Noelle had to keep from groaning. "You bet, Lucinda," she said brightly, feeling like the words were a lie as they came out of her mouth.

After they finished the conversation and she hung up, Noelle stayed in the vestibule, staring at the passersby in Asheville and hearing the raucous laughter of the family she loved behind her in the bridal salon.

What just happened, exactly?

Was Noelle's biggest professional dream essentially dead? A month ago, that would have crushed her. Today, it—

"Come on, Miss Noelle!" The demand was accompanied by a tiny seven-year-old hand smacking the glass door. "Bitsy has the first dress on, and she won't come out until you're here."

Noelle grabbed the handle and pulled the door open, reaching down to scoop up the child she loved so much. "I'm sorry, it was work."

"You work too much, Miss Noelle."

Out of the mouths of babes...

Aunt Elizabeth's first dress was an unmitigated disaster that resulted in so much laughter, Noelle's stomach hurt. The second dress was not so bad, but the cream tone looked yellow and none of them liked it. The third dress was for a much more matronly woman and, despite her fondness for overalls, Aunt Elizabeth still had a lovely figure that she shouldn't hide. The fourth dress was made for a mermaid and that was just all kinds of wrong.

"We don't have a lot of options left," the salon owner said as she ushered Elizabeth back to the dressing room. "Most of our brides come in six months in advance, so all I have is what I have, and alterations will have to be minor to be done in two days."

"Well, there's one more." Elizabeth paused before she disappeared behind the corner. "Say a prayer this one works, girls!"

"We will, just no more mermaids," Noelle called after her.

"I didn't hate the mermaid," Aunt Elizabeth said from the dressing room.

"We did!" they answered in unison, laughing.

"Just come on out and let us judge," Angie teased with a wink to the others. "We promise not to make any more jokes."

"No, we don't." Noelle gave a squeeze to the little

girl firmly planted on her lap. "Maybe a unicorn now that the mermaid look is over."

"I like unicorns."

Noelle laughed and kissed Cassie's head. "I know you do."

"Ladies." The salon owner came out a few minutes later, giving a flourish and a bow. "Dress number five."

They waited a beat, but Elizabeth didn't step out.

"Don't like it, Bitsy?" Angie called, glancing at the others with concern in her eyes.

"You can go with the mermaid if you want that one," Eve said, pushing up when she stayed out of sight.

All they heard was a sniffle.

"Aunt Elizabeth?" Noelle leaned forward, concern making her tighten her grip on Cassie. "Are you all right?"

With one more noisy sniffle, she stepped out into the salon, and the first thing Noelle noticed were her tears. The second? The dress that looked like it had been made exclusively for Elizabeth Whitaker to wear on her wedding day.

Chills and gasps, oohs, ahhs, and even some applause filled the initial shocked silence as Elizabeth slowly stepped up on the fitting stage. She held out her arms so they could see the pure white satin A-line gown with cap sleeves, a square neckline, and a short train.

Vera Wang couldn't have made a more perfect dress for her. It was elegant, classy, simple, clean, and achingly beautiful.

"Girls," Elizabeth whispered, sliding her hands into the folds. "It even has pockets! I found the dress I want to wear when I marry the man I've waited my entire life to find."

They exploded into cheers, more tears, plenty of toasts, and a group hug around the bride. There really wasn't much to say except, well, *yes to the dress.*

After the salon owner pinned the hem and an easy alteration in the waist, the woman turned to Cassie. "And I hear we have a little flower girl to dress as well. I have a few selected for you, young lady, in this other dressing room, if you're ready."

"I am!" Cassie popped off Noelle's lap, then turned, holding out her hand. "Come with me, Miss Noelle."

"Of course." As she let herself be led by the hand, Noelle looked back over her shoulder just in time to catch the look Eve and Angie shared in response to that.

A knowing look. A hopeful look. A loving sisterly look from two women who only wanted Noelle to be happy.

In the dressing room, Cassie spun and gasped as she stared at the three different dresses hanging for her, almost as overwhelmed as Elizabeth had been.

"Which one do you like the best, Cass?" Noelle asked.

"The light pink one with the fluffy bottom. It looks like a princess."

"Why am I not surprised?" Noelle reached for the hanger. "Do you want some help?"

"I want to see you in a wedding dress."

Noelle blinked at the announcement. "Well, I'm not the one buying a dress today." Unless she meant the dress Noelle would wear to the wedding. "After this, we're all going to another shop to buy our dresses for the wedding, but this one is just for brides and attendants."

"No, I mean a white gown like Aunt Bitsy."

Noelle sighed and tipped her head. "It's not my day, sweetheart." She lifted the dress from the hanger. "But it's yours, so do you want to—"

"Don't you want to marry my daddy?"

Noelle bit her lip, her eyes shuttering as she lowered herself to get eye-to-eye with Cassie. "Baby girl, that's a big, big decision and no one makes it easily."

"But will you marry him? Ever?" Her eyes grew more serious than usual. This mattered to her, and that made Noelle's heart hurt. "I want you to be my—"

She stopped her with a light touch of her fingers to Cassie's lips. "Shhh. Don't say it."

"Why not?"

"Because we're in early days, darling. Your father and I just reconnected this month. This isn't the movies. People don't change their lives that quickly."

"But don't you love him?"

"I..." She couldn't say the words to Jace, but could

she say them to Cassie? "I think so," she finally whispered. "But I don't know for sure yet."

Cassie stared at her, eyes the same gray-blue as her father's growing wide and wet. "But I love you, Miss Noelle."

"Oh, honey." She reached and hugged her. "I love you, too. And I want you to know that your dad and I have real feelings. We're going to keep being friends and talking every day when I go back to New York. I'll FaceTime you and you'll fly up to New York to visit me and...and..."

She waited for the burst of happiness at this plan, the big Cassie enthusiasm for the possibility of a trip to New York.

But the little girl just stared at her.

"And I'll come here to Asheville all the time," Noelle finished. "I promise."

Outside, the salon owner tapped on the door. "How's it going in there, ladies?"

"We better hurry up and get dressed," Noelle said. "Fluffy bottom?"

Cassie nodded. "I can do it," she said, her voice all tight and grown up. "You wait outside and tie the bow."

As she stepped out of the dressing room, Noelle could hear the chatter from the women in the salon, but all she could think about was how invested Cassie was. How hurt she'd be if this relationship didn't work out, and how even a long-distance romance could be hard for her. For all of them.

Aunt Elizabeth came around the corner, back in

her overalls, which looked so good and right on her, as beautiful as the dress.

"Did she find one?" she asked.

Noelle nodded, not trusting her voice, because her throat was so tight with unshed tears.

"The poofy princess?"

Noelle laughed at that. "Of course," she whispered, forcing herself not to cry. "I love the dress you picked. It's perfection."

"Not exactly Chanel," Elizabeth joked. "But I'm happy."

"Ah, yes, Chanel." Noelle tipped her head, remembering that she and Jace were going to Charlotte to get the designer gloves that would be perfect with this dress. "Well, those days are behind you."

Elizabeth put a light hand on Noelle's cheek. "Seasons change, my dearest darling. Old ones end and new ones start."

"Yep. And you know how I feel about change." Noelle smiled. "Not my favorite pastime."

"Change is scary," she said. "But it can be so, so good."

She blew out a breath. "My boss might be taking over the London office."

Elizabeth frowned. "What does that mean for your five-year plan to run that operation?"

"It was a two-year plan, but this means I might have to wait *ten* years to ever prance down Abbey Road or shop at Harrods." Noelle shrugged. "And maybe that's just fine."

"Maybe it is," Elizabeth said.

"I'm ready!" The dressing room door opened, and Cassie stepped out in her pale pink princess dress and twirled. "Can you tie the bow, Miss Noelle?"

"I sure can." Noelle bent over and tugged the wide satin ribbon, forming a beautiful bow, then gave Cassie's shoulders a squeeze. "You look just like a princess," she whispered.

As Cassie swept by to skip her way to the platform and get her well-deserved applause, Noelle hung back with Elizabeth.

"How do you know when the path is clear?" she asked her aunt, desperate for answers and direction. "How do you know?"

Elizabeth smiled. "Your heart will sing."

"Okay." She pressed a hand on her chest, hoping she would hear every note if and when her heart sang.

Chapter Nine

Eve

THE WORDS of the novel Eve was trying to read in bed kept blurring and boring her. There was nothing wrong with the book. She was simply having a terrible time concentrating on anything but the seed that had germinated in her heart since she'd met with Gabby.

Adoption. Was the idea even worth thinking about?

On a long sigh, she darkened her e-reader and lowered it, glancing at David, who was watching a video on his phone.

"Exhausted from all the dress shopping?" he asked, clicking off the phone and reaching to set it on the nightstand. "You've been so quiet."

"Yeah, I'm tired with all the wedding planning and...stuff."

He eyed her, turning to face her. "You've been busy, that's for sure. The decorations, the dresses, all the wedding business. I've been busy, too." He lifted a brow. "That conversation with Amir went really well and the ball is rolling."

He'd been in a great mood after his conversation

with Amir Patel, the doctor who headed his neuro-surgery group in Charlotte. Though Amir had been shocked at the decision, he was supportive and grateful that David assured him the transition would be smooth.

"It's awesome that you'll help find your own replacement."

"Which won't take long," he said. "I'd still like to be settled, moved, and in our new life by summer, latest."

She nodded, gnawing on her lip as she tried to find a graceful way to bring up the subject of Gabby...and the baby.

He narrowed his eyes, studying her. "You're still okay with that?"

"Of course. Why?"

"Because you're quiet. Pensive. And not...Evie."

She chuckled at that. "Well, I'm...thinking about some things."

"About having another baby?" he guessed.

She nodded, rooting around for how to start, waiting for the perfect lead-in to bring up the possibility of adoption.

"What worries you the most?" he asked.

"Oh, I guess my age and the whole pregnancy thing, for starters."

"None of our babies were difficult to conceive," he reminded her. "We weren't even trying for Sawyer."

"But I'm forty, and you're forty-three."

"I've been reading a lot of medical journals on conception and pregnancy in your forties and, honestly, honey, it's not a huge deal. But if you don't want to—"

"I want a baby," she interjected. "I'm just..." She let her voice trail off, imagining his reaction. David was practical, logical, and unemotional. Something told her he wouldn't be over the moon about adopting a baby from a woman who was single, young, and nine months pregnant.

Maybe she needed a little practicality and logic on the subject.

Taking a breath, she put her e-reader on the night-stand and turned to him, searching his face to gauge how open and awake he might be. Was this a good time?

Good heavens, Gabby could be going into labor tonight. It *had* to be a good time.

"Can I talk to you about something super serious?" she asked.

He eased back, his expression a mix of surprise and hurt. "Why would you even ask me that? Of course. And, hey, if you're thinking this whole move to Hendersonville and change in jobs is too much, I get that. I want you to be happy, honey. I'm excited about the change—freakishly so—but only if you are."

She smiled. "I'm freakishly excited, too," she told him. "But the serious thing I want to talk to you about is...adoption."

His brows flickered at the word, and she saw a bunch of emotions flash on his face, gone before she could analyze any of them.

"Okay," he finally said. "What about it?"

"You know that girl I had lunch with, Gabby? You know she's very, very pregnant."

He stared at her, not nodding, not reacting, just waiting.

"Like, she's due now."

"And..."

"And we did not talk about this at all, I swear," she said, sitting up a little to make sure she could get her thoughts out properly. "Well, she made a joke about giving me the baby to raise and the second she said it...something..." She tapped her chest. "Something happened in here. And I started thinking...maybe that would be the way to go."

"Adoption." He said the word slowly, as if it took a whole lot of getting used to. As if he'd never considered it and probably didn't love the idea.

"Well, adopting her baby, specifically."

He blinked and sat up, too. "A baby about to be born?"

"If we wait, she might end up going through another adoption or she might keep it and try to raise it alone. She's all alone, David. No mother, no husband. It feels like Dr. Robinson is her only friend in the world."

"Eve. Let's start with the fact that we know nothing about her. Zero. She could take drugs or drink or—"

"She's very healthy. Doesn't drink and doesn't eat sushi and—"

"We know nothing about the father, either."

She couldn't argue that. "We know Terrance, her

doctor. I'm sure he could vouch for her health, and maybe he knows the father."

"He won't break patient confidentiality and, frankly, it would be wrong of me to ask."

"If you're adopting her baby?"

He stared at her for a moment, clearly dumbstruck. "You're serious," he said after a beat. "You would really consider adopting when we make the world's most amazing kids?"

"How much is nature and how much is nurture?" she countered. "We *raised* the world's most amazing kids, and they might all be ours, but they couldn't be more different."

"But is she putting the baby up for adoption? Because that paperwork and process should have been done a long time ago. There could be a waiting list for that baby."

"She's undecided," Eve said. "Part of her wants to keep the baby, which is what stopped her from terminating when her boyfriend wanted her to."

"And where's he?"

"Gone. Living in a van."

"Great," David scoffed.

"I think she's had preliminary conversations with adoption agencies—I'm really not sure. She got into NC State and wants to go in the fall, but has no idea how she could do that with a baby."

"What if she wants the baby back after college? What if she changes her mind? What if this breaks your heart, Eve?"

She looked at him, fighting tears, mostly because he was right. "I suppose that's a risk," she said. "But when the idea landed in my head, all I know is it felt really, really right. Like someone had put that young woman in my path because she's carrying *our* baby. Is that completely crazy?"

"Yeah," he said, but tempered the response with a laugh. "But I learned a long time ago not to fight your instincts. They're usually right."

She smiled at that. "It was when she talked about how much she wanted her baby to have a life like the one we've built for our boys that really got me thinking. She wants to do what's right for her little girl and—"

"It's a girl? She's sure?"

Eve nodded. "Perfectly healthy, too. Could you ask Terrance about the baby? Would that break confidentiality?"

He thought about that for a minute—or maybe about the whole idea—finally falling back on his pillow as the impact hit him.

"Maybe. Wow. Adoption. That's...interesting."

The first glimmer of hope sparked in her chest. "It could be amazing."

"It could be...not amazing," he volleyed.

"Would you meet her?" she asked.

He didn't answer right away, but crossed his hands on his chest and stared at the ceiling in a classic David Gallagher thinking pose. She could practically hear the wheels turning in his head, and imagined all those pros and cons being lined up and weighed out.

What was right for the family; what was good for Eve; what was best for the baby; what were the emotional, psychological, physical, and financial considerations.

David did not make big decisions lightly, so she slowly slid back down under the covers on her side, watching his great brain do all the work.

Finally, he turned to her. "I'll meet her."

She whooshed out a breath she hadn't realized she'd been holding, suddenly reaching to hug him, a little shocked at how much this meant to her. She'd been tamping down her enthusiasm for the idea and trying to bury the possibility as something that should be ignored.

"Before we do that," she said, "I need to have a conversation with her. She has no idea I'm thinking about this. And if she's agreeable, then you should meet her."

"I'd like that. Sooner, if possible. Before she has the baby."

"Oh." She bit her lip and let out a little whimper of joy. "Thank you, David!"

"Evie." He wrapped her in his arms, pulling her close. "You really want this, don't you?"

"I guess...I might. I don't know. But what I don't want is to be in it alone anymore. I want to talk to her, and we'll take it from there. Maybe she'll let us go to her next appointment with Terrance. I don't know if it can all happen that fast, but it feels so, so right to me."

He nodded, his eyes suddenly misty. "I can see that," he said, his voice thick.

"David? Are you upset? Are you mad? Do you not want to—"

"Shh. I just love you." He voice was thick, proving that her very logical physician husband had an emotional side of his own. "I love your heart and soul, Evie. I love how much you're concerned for others and what a great mother you are and...will be."

"Aww, thank you. You're a great father, too. And I think that little baby, if her mother decides to part with her and we decide it's the right thing for our family, would be very lucky to land in the Gallagher family."

He just sighed and held her close, and they stayed that way, quiet until they slept.

GABBY AGREED to coffee the next morning, answering Eve's text right away. Slipping out of the house was easy, since everyone else seemed preoccupied with what they had to do that day. Noelle was off to finish off the "somethings" for the wedding, taking a day trip to Charlotte with Jace, and Angie was totally focused on meeting Garrett Delacorte at Biltmore House that day.

No one but David knew where Eve was going when she took his car and made the now-familiar drive down to Hendersonville. The whole way down, her mind was spinning with a million questions for Gabby, with a lot of David's issues tapping at her heart, too.

She didn't want to get swept up into a fantasy that made no sense or could blow up in her face. She had to be honest with Gabby and get a real sense of how serious she was regarding adoption. Then she could pepper her with questions about health and history. Or maybe she should do it the other way around.

Still uncertain how to proceed, Eve found Black Bear Coffee—stopping to take a picture of the giant black bear for Sawyer, who'd yet to see a real one after nearly four weeks of trying—and stepped into the warm, cinnamon and coffee-scented diner.

Ordering a latte that would probably do nothing to calm her nerves, she snagged a table at the front with a view of the door, and was halfway through her cup when Gabby finally came in.

"Late as usual," Gabby said with a laugh as she untied her scarf. "It's my fatal flaw, I'm afraid."

"Well, if that's your worst trait..." Eve started to say something about how that boded well for the baby, but caught herself. "Well, that's not a very bad one."

"I try to get to places on time—I was never late for work. But I always think I have more time than I do." She slipped into the chair and patted her sizeable belly. "If she's inherited it, we'll know if she misses her due date."

"How do you feel?" Eve asked, leaning forward and wishing she knew the young woman well enough to take her hand. "No more Braxton Hicks?"

"Some, but they pass really quickly. I'm not sleeping well, but I guess I'll have to get used to that." She sighed as if the idea didn't thrill her.

"Can I order you something to drink?" Eve asked, tipping her head toward the coffee bar.

"Hot chocolate," she said, pushing back. "I'll get—"

"Nonsense. Stay here. I'll get it for you. Whipped cream? Anything special?"

"Yes, whipped cream, and thank you, Eve," she said warmly, a real light in her eyes. "You're really kind."

Eve just smiled, hoping Gabby still thought that after she found out why Eve had invited her here.

A few minutes later, Gabby was using a spoon to enjoy the mound of whipped cream on her hot chocolate, suddenly seeming as young as one of Eve's boys when faced with a sweet treat.

After some small-talk, Eve took a breath and decided not to dive right into a discussion about adoption. Gabby seemed so comfortable, not questioning the coffee date, and even happy. Not that Eve's idea should make her *un*happy, but she wanted to tread lightly.

So she tried to think of ways for Gabby to share her health history and lifestyle.

"Good thing they haven't taken chocolate away from pregnant women," she said casually. "It does seem like every time you turn around, there's another thing you can't do, eat, or drink when you're pregnant."

"Tell me about it," Gabby said. "No allergy meds—which I need, because I have terrible allergies when the weather changes. I've wiped fish out of my diet, no fake sweeteners, two extra washes on the fruit, and have you heard no deli meat?"

"No! Why?"

"Fear of listeria."

Eve nodded, so grateful Gabby was on top of her health game. "Of course, you don't drink," she said. "Or...anything else."

Gabby shook her head. "No, I don't drink. Or anything else. I want to study nutrition, remember? I'm kind of obsessed with it, although you could never tell by the way I'm sucking down this whipped cream."

"It's comfort food," Eve said with a light laugh of relief, deciding to drop the health food issue. There were too many other questions. "So, uh, Gabby. Are you in touch with the baby's father at all? I know you said he lives in a van, but do you think he's out of the picture for good?"

She lifted a shoulder. "He offered me some money, but he doesn't have much. We weren't, you know, forever."

Eve nodded. "What's he like?"

"Kyle?" Another shrug. "He's actually a really gifted artist. He works with metal and stone and makes beautiful things. And he's kind of an adventurer, always looking for the next good time. He was talking about taking a year in Japan if he could afford it. He's not a bad guy. Just not interested in being a father at all."

"Do you think that might change after she's born?"

Because Eve certainly didn't want to adopt a baby only to have the father demand to take her away.

"No. I can't tell you how much he doesn't want to be a dad."

"But after she's born? After he's...seen her?"

She shook her head, sadness in her eyes. "He doesn't want to be in her life. And that's fine. I wasn't in love with him, I'm sad to say."

Eve nodded. "What about your mother?"

"What about her?"

"You don't have any relationship with her?"

"None whatsoever. I haven't talked to the woman in years, and I don't even know if she's dead or alive. And before you judge, that was her choice, her decision."

"I'm not judging."

"Well, you're asking a lot of questions." She shifted in her seat, uncomfortable. "I haven't asked you anything."

"You can," Eve said. "And I don't mean to pry, but..."

"But what?" Gabby frowned, leaning forward. "Are you undercover with Child Services or something? Why are you grilling me?"

"I'm not, no, I'm not." Eve huffed out a breath. "I'm very interested in...you."

"Why?"

Eve closed her eyes. "Okay, I have to ask you one more question, Gabby. And I want you to be honest and understand that this comes from a place of love."

She backed away, her entire expression defensive and scared. "What?"

"How serious are you about giving up your baby for adoption?"

The response was dead silence and a long, indecipherable look.

"Because you made a comment—maybe it was a joke—about me and...well, you did say you were considering adoption and I—well, David and I—have been talking for a while about another baby and..." She swallowed and silently pleaded for an answer, but didn't get one. "I thought maybe you were put in my path for a reason," she finally finished. "And I wanted to just talk to you about the possibility. No pressure, no commitments, no anything. Just talk."

Gabby's shoulders sank a little as she exhaled. "Oh." It was all she said, and Eve had no idea if that was a good *Oh* or a bad *Oh*.

Eve closed her eyes and leaned forward. "Feel free to tell me to get lost."

"No, no, I...don't want to say that," she said haltingly. "I just...I don't know."

"Of course you don't. It's a massive decision, you've known me for a day or two, and we're talking about a life that is so precious you have turned yours upside down to bring her into the world."

She gave an unsteady smile. "I like that you noticed that."

Eve leaned over the table and put a hand over Gabby's. "There's no rush and no decision to be made.

The only thing I wanted to do is plant the seed, like you did."

"I did?"

"When you said too bad I didn't want to adopt her. That you thought I'd be a good mother."

She nodded, biting on her lower lip.

"If you didn't mean that or you are not in any way even considering adoption, then please forgive me for overstepping. I just—"

"I don't know," she interjected. "I don't hate the idea, but I don't love it, either."

Eve nodded, not answering, because she sensed she was finally going to get Gabby's true feelings.

"I kept thinking through the whole pregnancy that I'd know the answer," she said. "I thought the answer would be completely clear. I've been looking for a sign."

Somehow Eve resisted saying, "I am the sign!" and kept her hand on Gabby's, silent.

"I figured I'd wake up one day and know—I want to keep this baby or I want to give this baby up for adoption. But I don't know. What's best for her, what's best for me? I don't know."

"You don't have anyone you can talk to about it?" Eve asked.

"I have two girlfriends. Well, one is an older woman I worked with at the diner. She said to keep it. And my other girlfriend is kind of a partier, so she's like, give it up and be young! I'm only twenty," she added softly. "I'm not sure I'd be a very good mother. I do have my own mother's craptastic genes, so who knows? Maybe I'd meet a man and up and leave her when she's five." Her voice cracked and Eve added pressure to her touch.

"No, you wouldn't. Those aren't genes, Gabby, they're life decisions. And you're facing a big one. I'm kind of biased, obviously, but I'll answer your questions. I'll help you make a decision, and I won't encourage adoption if I don't think it's right. I promise."

Gabby nodded. "You told me a lot about your family, your husband, your boys. And I can tell you're awesome, but...why wouldn't you just have a baby of your own?"

Eve finally lifted her hand, leaning back to consider her response. "I could, but I don't know if I should. David, my husband, and I are definitely talking about it. We both want another baby, but I'm forty and I don't know if it would be easy to conceive or carry. After we had dinner, I started thinking about what you'd said, and it just felt right. I don't have any better explanation except the very idea just sits on my heart like it was meant to be. Does that make sense?"

Gabby exhaled again and gave a slight smile, placing a hand on her stomach. "Baby Girl is moving."

"Oh? Isn't that the best feeling?"

She smiled and blinked back some tears. "I just don't know, Eve. Can I think about it? I need to think."

"Of course. Gabby, please. There's no rush, none at all. Well, I suppose there's a bit of a rush, but I'm here for you. And for your baby girl."

She pushed back, holding up a hand so that Eve didn't stand, too. "I need some time."

"I understand."

Hastily pulling on her coat and throwing her scarf over her shoulders, she nodded, tears welling. "Thank you for the hot chocolate and...everything. Thank you."

With that, she hustled out, and all Eve could do was sigh and wonder if she hadn't just completely blown it.

Chapter Ten

Angie

"I GUESS it's time to meet the devil himself," Angie said to Brooke as they trudged up a hill in downtown Asheville, headed to the understated Biltmore Estate corporate headquarters.

"And the devil's son," Brooke added as she blew into her hands to ward off the severe and sudden drop in temperature. "Although, for the record, he's been very nice when we talk."

Angie stopped mid-step. "You've actually *talked* to Sam Delacorte?"

"We've texted, which, in teenagespeak, is talking. You know that, Mom."

"Maybe, but talking is talking."

"Actually, 'talking' can be the preliminary step to dating." At Angie's stunned look, Brooke laughed. "I'm just teaching you the lingo, Mom. In this case, talking is casually texting, because we have this weird connection and knew we'd see each other today."

"So he came all the way from Miami just to meet you."

"On a private plane."

"Oh, please." Angie rolled her eyes. "What does this horrible man need with our little property on Copper Creek Mountain? It's preposterous."

"Sam just said his dad is super competitive because he's the youngest of all these rich overachievers and one of his brothers was on the team that—"

"Invented the Nintendo...something. I remember. Angie's boys freaked out."

Brooke laughed. "The sixty-four. Yeah, well, according to Sam, that's at the root of everything his dad does. He's been through two wives, a few girlfriends, several companies, and doesn't speak to his oldest daughter."

"Oh, he sounds like a lovely man." She rolled her eyes.

Brooke snorted a laugh. "Not at all. But Sam seems cool. But then, so did Vance when I started *talking* to him and then he turned out to be a secret society freak." Brooke looked up at the stairs and the entrance to the building. "Let's just be on our guard, Mom. Don't lose your cool with this guy."

"I'm always cool," Angie said, squaring her shoulders like she was headed into battle. "I'm cucumber cool. I'm LL Cool Angie. I'm so cool, you need a heater around me. I'm—"

"Got it." Brooke put a hand on her back. "Now zip it."

Angie fought a laugh as they opened the heavy

glass door and instantly saw Marjorie Summerall in the small reception area.

"Hello, Angie." She reached out for a light hug, which Angie took as a sign that no matter what happened with Garrett Delacorte, Marjorie was on her side.

"And Brooke." Marjorie reached out both hands. "So lovely to see you again. Not as grand here as the House, though." She gestured toward the clean and simple lines of a business environment. "I hope you won't be bored."

"I'm good, Ms. Summerall," Brooke replied, her level of deference and respect giving Angie a jolt of affection for her daughter.

"And I so appreciate you both coming just days before your aunt's wedding and this week between Christmas and New Year's. And it looks like we're getting a heavy snowfall, too, but we should be out of here before the worst of it. The offices are officially closed, so you won't see many people, but I scheduled this thinking you'd be back in California after the holidays."

"I might be," Angie said dryly. "If our buddy Garrett doesn't back off."

Marjorie winced. "He's in the conference room with his son, Sam." She brightened and looked at Brooke. "He's about your age, honey, so maybe you'll hit it off."

Brooke just smiled, not giving away the fact that she and Sam were "talking" but not "talking."

"How is Garrett?" Angie asked, leaning in a bit. "Friendly? Kind? Ready to acknowledge this is all a big mistake?"

"Oh, Angie, I wish we'd have known how this would unfold," she said. "We could have had you record separately. The timing is terrible."

Angie shrugged, noticing that Marjorie didn't exactly answer her question.

"I don't suppose you, uh, scared up a surprise deed I could wave in his face?" she asked.

"Nothing, but I am in touch with the man who keeps the original butler's logs from back in the day. He's out of the country on vacation right now, but when he calls me, I'm hoping there will be something—anything at all—recorded that might help you. Other than that, nothing."

"It's fine, I understand. Ever onward and all that."

Marjorie smiled and ushered them toward the back offices and up a set of stairs.

Behind her, Angie and Brooke shared a silent look, with maybe a little warning in Brooke's eyes.

"What?" Angie mouthed, totally silent. "I'm so cool."

Brooke looked skyward and they followed the other woman down a short hallway.

"Have you ever done a podcast, Angie? Or a radio interview?" Marjorie asked as they reached a closed door with frosted glass that prevented them from seeing inside.

"Uh, no." Should she have? Was it normal to have

not done a podcast? "I listen to them, though," she added brightly.

Marjorie smiled. "You'll wear a headset and speak into a mic. There's a tech in there who'll guide you through the narration. I take it you read the script we sent? Because you can't make any changes now."

"Read it and memorized it," she said as Marjorie opened the door. With one more look to Brooke, Angie whispered, "See? I can be an overachiever, too."

"Cool, Mom. Be cool."

As they stepped inside the dimly lit, windowless room, Angie sucked in a breath and scanned the three faces, knowing instantly which one was Satan himself. He sat at the head of the table. Looking to be in his mid-to-late fifties, he had a narrow face, stark features, and closely cropped brown hair.

No surprise, he didn't even look up from his phone.

The technician behind a small recording console set up on the table stood, brushing back shoulder-length hair to greet them. And the boy who looked a little younger than sixteen also stood, instantly putting down his phone—proving he had more class than his wealthy father.

"This is Angie and Brooke Messina," Marjorie announced. "Better known as the great-granddaughter and great-great-granddaughter of Angelica and Garland Benson, former staff members at Biltmore House. And, of course," she added as Garrett finally looked up and met Angie's gaze, "Angelica is the reason we're all here."

"Well, Claudia Winchester is," Garrett said, his thin lips not lifting in anything remotely resembling a smile. "Not to put too fine a point on it."

Angie sucked in a soft breath, the response to that screaming in her head.

Claudia Winchester would have perished in a fire if Angelica Benson hadn't risked her life to save the child!

But, true to her new cool self, she merely offered a humorless smile and shook the technician's hand, got that his name was Rick, and then turned to Sam.

"Hello, Mrs. Messina," the young man said, offering his hand and a sweet smile. He had light brown hair, a little shaggy but not too long, and the same angular features as his father. On him, they looked like youth that might blossom into handsome. On his father? Just sharp edges.

"Sam, is it? How nice of you to come for this."

"It's fun," he said. "I'd never been to Biltmore House before, and we got the full private tour this morning."

She drew back, knowing her eyes must have flashed. "Never? And it's such a major part of your family's history."

"Which *you* didn't know until a month ago," Garrett said, the comment so soft she almost didn't hear it.

But it told her everything she needed to know about the evil, rotten, selfish man. He was going to fight dirty.

Her heart dropping—and her daughter watching—

Angie responded with a smile. "And what glorious news it was." She took a seat at the opposite end of the table, hoping that looked like a power move.

She turned to Rick. "So, what do we need to do?"

"Here's your script," he said, sliding a few pieces of paper to her. "We'll do your lead-in first, then Mr. Delacorte, then you talk again, then he does. Having you both in the room is awesome from an editing perspective."

Well, it sure wasn't awesome from any other perspective. But Angie nodded and took the headphones, sliding them over her ears, and watched in silence as Rick placed a wired microphone on a stand in front of her.

"We can do as many takes as you like," Rick said.

"Or as few," Garrett said. "I'd like to be done in fifteen minutes, if that's possible. You may all treat this week like a vacation, but I have six businesses to run."

Gah. She hated him but refused to even bristle. "I'm sure we can do it in one take," Angie said.

"Let's start with a soundcheck." Rick nodded toward her mic. "Say anything at all, I just want to level your voice."

"Anything?" She slid a look to Brooke, who was sitting in the chair next to Sam, across from the technician. She just narrowed her eyes in warning at Angie.

"Usually your name, birthday, something about yourself so I can get a good ten or twelve seconds to set volume," Rick said.

"Okay." She cleared her throat and took a breath.

"My name is Angie Messina and I'm a triplet, born on Christmas Day."

At least that got the ogre to look up with a flicker of interest.

The tech circled his finger like he needed more.

She nodded. "I was named after my great-grand-mother, the wonderful woman who brings us all here today." She didn't know that she was named after Angelica for a fact, but since this wasn't a deposition, she felt okay stretching the truth.

Bonehead looked back at his phone, interest gone.

"That's good," Rick said. "Want to just read through once without recording?"

"No," Garrett said. "Just record and let me out of this windowless dungeon."

Marjorie, who'd taken a seat at the side of the room, leaned forward. "Would you like a break for air, Mr. Delacorte?"

"I'd like my life back. Carry on, please."

Rick gave a quick nod, pressed a few buttons, and pointed to Angie. "Go," he mouthed.

Oh, boy. She looked down at the script, which she really had memorized, but suddenly she was swamped with feelings. Memories. Agony. All the years of Craig's snide comments and sideways insults and constant reminders that he was better than she was.

And this arrogant jerk was doing exactly the same thing!

She took a breath, closed her eyes, and dug for steadiness and—

"Any day now," Garrett said under his breath.

Looking up at him, rage nearly rocked her, but then she felt Brooke's presence and that had the opposite effect.

With a smile, she started to read. "Welcome to the servants' quarters on the fourth floor of Biltmore House," she said, happy that her voice was smooth and steady. "These halls housed the higher-level staff who served the needs of the Vanderbilt family and their guests. The first room on your right is the only servants' bedroom that was big enough for two people, and was home to a happily married couple named Angelica and Garland Benson. Garland was a footman for many years in the household, and Angelica, his wife, was a parlor maid. They were also my great-grandparents." She took a breath and a beat, feeling it now. "My name is Angie Chambers..." She hesitated for a nanosecond, then made the sudden decision to drop her married name. It was history anyway. "And I'm delighted to share some personal history while you tour this room."

The split-second decision to drop Messina gave her exactly the injection of confidence she needed, and a quick look of approval from Brooke underscored that it was the right thing to do.

Rick turned to Garrett. "Uh, Mr. Delacorte. You're up."

He seemed surprised, putting down his precious phone and taking the paper with a frown. He cleared his throat before speaking. "And my name is Garrett Delacorte, the grandson of one of the Vanderbilts' most prestige...prestigious...pres—" He grunted and shook his head after stumbling on the pronunciation. "Start again, please."

Oh, sure, Mr. One Take.

Angie just smiled, like she had all the patience and time in the world.

On his last line, he mistakenly said "Garner" instead of "Garland" and they had to start all over again.

That made him swear and scowl.

"This could take a while," Sam said softly to Brooke. "Want to go get a coffee?"

Brooke seemed surprised by the invitation, but Garrett jumped in and answered for her.

"Yes, please," he said gruffly. "We don't need an audience for this."

Angie gave her a nod, hoping it was enough to communicate that she felt confident and, yes, cool, and Brooke and Sam grabbed their coats and stepped out.

"Pick up on your second 'graph," Rick instructed Angie.

She nodded, and this time, as she read the words she'd committed to memory, she stared right into the evil eyes of her nemesis.

"Angelica's most eventful day as a parlor maid was January 10, 1924, when a small fire broke out in one of the guest rooms downstairs. Angelica was working when she smelled the smoke and realized that a small child, Claudia Winchester, the daughter of distant relatives who were visiting the Vanderbilts, was asleep in her crib in the room where the fire started." She held Garrett's gaze with one of her own, intense enough that even he couldn't look away as she reminded him—and the world—that her great-grandmother saved the life of his grandmother.

"Using her apron to cover her mouth, Angelica rushed headlong into the smoky room where the curtains above the sleeping baby's head were already ablaze. She reached into the crib and pulled out the four-month-old infant and carried her out of the room to safety."

Garrett stayed silent, even after Rick turned to give him his cue. Then he leaned forward, casting his gaze down to the script, which he obviously had *not* memorized.

"Claudia Winchester went on to live a long and storied life, which included a stint as a spy in World War II, and working side by side with her husband, Frank Delacorte, a speechwriter for President Dwight D. Eisenhower. She had six grandchildren, of which I am one."

He waited a beat, both of them staring at the next line, which read, "Another was instrumental in the invention of the Nintendo 64."

But he didn't say the words. Instead, he closed his eyes, and read the line after that.

"All of her children are grateful for the courage of the woman who, along with her husband, lived and worked at Biltmore House."

Wow, he is a small and jealous man, Angie thought.

Petty and pathetic. Spurred by that thought, she leaned into her microphone and spoke again.

"Louise and Keegan Winchester, Claudia's parents, were so grateful," she added, going off script but not caring, "that they gifted the Bensons with a piece of property outside of Asheville, where they built a home that is still part of their family's legacy to this very day." She ground out the last few words, knowing she wasn't exactly cool, but didn't care one bit.

The man across the table merely sighed like she was nothing but a nuisance.

She gripped the microphone and continued. "Wasn't that kind and generous of the Winchesters? They knew that the Bensons and their descendants would always have a home and the memory of Angelica's bravery. They wanted to be sure that a hundred years later, that home would still be filled with family and love, which it is today. Of course, if she hadn't risked her life, there wouldn't *be* a Delacorte family—"

Garrett shot to his feet. "We're done here."

"Uh, actually, I am not done." Angie stood, too, pointing at him. "Do you have any idea what you're doing? It might be a title to you, a land grab, a way to make your already swelling portfolio—and ego—even bigger, but it is my family's home."

"Please," he scoffed. "For twenty-five years it's either been vacant or a vacation rental. Get off your high horse about your family's legacy. Before this month, when was the last time you were there?"

She just stared at him, hating that he and his stupid lawyer knew so much.

She swallowed. "It was vacant because my sisters and I were there when my parents were killed in a car accident. It's been hard, but this year we—"

"Spare me the sob story."

"Seriously?"

Marjorie, who'd been standing silent for the exchange, held up a hand. "This is most uncomfortable—"

"Then get out," Garrett said. When Angie gasped and Marjorie drew back in shock, he merely flicked his hand to the door. "Leave me alone with Ms. Messina or Chambers or whatever she wants to call herself. We need five minutes of privacy."

Marjorie gave Angie an uncertain look, but Angie nodded. "I'll talk to him alone. It's okay."

"And after that, I'm done," Garrett said to Rick. "So use what you have and don't come asking for more recordings."

What a jerk!

Rick and Marjorie's expressions said they agreed as they walked out of the room and left Angie and Garrett staring at each other.

She kept her back straight, her chin up, and refused to cower in the face of his dark, dark glare.

"How much?" he finally asked.

"Excuse me?"

"How much to get you off my back and let me have the property? I'll pay you."

Her whole body bristled at the words. "You'll...pay me? The property is not for sale."

"I'm not buying it, Angie," he snarled. "I already own it."

"You don't have a deed," she fired back.

"Well, neither do you."

"You don't know that."

His eyes widened. "Then what are you waiting for? Show it and get this over with. You do not have a deed."

She crossed her arms and stared at him, not speaking because she didn't want to lie.

"Now, back to my original question," he said. "How much to get rid of you and tear down that atrocity so I can build something that will generate real income?"

Her jaw dropped so hard and so fast, she could have sworn it hit her chest.

Tear it down?

"I'll be generous," he said.

"I don't care if you hand me ten million dollars—"

He snorted. "I was thinking a lot less."

"Because that home means something to a lot of people. And it's where I plan to live with my daughter, and where we will spend every single Christmas together until...until...there are grandkids and great-grandkids. Forever and ever, and you cannot put a price on that kind of family happiness."

He grunted with disgust and scooped up his phone. "Fine. Turn down my offer, I don't care. You have three days and that house and everything in it will be leveled."

With that, he walked out and slammed the door.

For a moment, she couldn't move or breathe or think or do anything but hear the echo of his words.

That house and everything in it will be leveled.

"Why?" she whispered to herself. There was nothing wrong with the cabin, especially since Aunt Elizabeth renovated and remodeled it. It was worth a tidy sum to rent or buy. Why would he destroy it?

"Mom?" Brooke burst into the room. "Are you okay?"

She slowly dropped into the chair and stared straight ahead. "He wants to level the house."

"And I know why."

Angie whipped around. "Why?"

Brooke took the seat the tech had abandoned and leaned in. "Sam—super sweet, by the way—told me something."

"What?"

"He heard his father say that he knows for a fact that the deed is in the house."

She stared at Brooke, her brain flipping through every inch and corner and drawer and shelf they'd already checked. "What if it went out in that antique desk and is lost forever?"

"I don't know, but Sam said he heard Garrett say the deed was hidden in the house—that was the word he used—*hidden*."

"How would he know that?"

Brooke raised her brow. "Apparently, it has to do with the stipulations that were in the deal when the

Winchesters gifted the land. That the deed stay with the house. Does that make any sense?"

"None at all, but you know what does make sense?" Angie asked.

Brooke nodded. "That he wants to destroy the house—and the deed—so you can never claim it."

"We are going to find that deed, Brooke Messina." Angie stood, on fire with determination. "We are going to find it and then I'm going to smash it in his smug, arrogant, obnoxious face and laugh."

Brooke smiled. "I like LL Cool Angie."

"Oh, baby, you ain't seen nothin' yet."

Chapter Eleven

Noelle

THE DAY in Charlotte had been lovely, if cold. From the moment Jace and Noelle climbed in the truck and left Asheville, they'd had a great time.

They spent the two-hour drive through rural and gorgeous North Carolina talking about everything and nothing, never once having anything that felt like an awkward moment. With each passing mile, they shared memories, experiences, viewpoints, and many, many laughs.

Then, in the bustling town, they'd gone from one high-end store to another, looking for Chanel gloves. Dependable, charming Jace in his flannel and country-boy smile had been a fish out of Nieman-Marcus waters, but they'd had fun searching for the perfect accessory, especially now that Noelle knew the dress.

They had lunch, did a little touring, and took a drive by Eve's house. She'd texted a picture to Eve, who offered to give them the code to get in, which was tempting. But Jace saw in the forecast that there was a lot of snow on the way, so they opted to get back on the highway and drive home before it got too heavy.

"Well, we should go try to visit Eve's house at some point," Noelle said as they rolled along the highway. "They won't be there long. She said she and David found an open house for a new build in Hendersonville that they're going to see tomorrow."

"Wow, they really are making this move," Jace said, shaking his head as he flipped the windshield wipers faster as the snow fell. "But that house we drove by was really nice. Whatever they get for it, they can buy something great in Hendersonville."

"He won't have a brain surgeon's income, though," Noelle reminded him.

"Huh." Jace shot her a look. "Look at that. Guy's changing his whole career, even taking what some might consider a step down professionally, all for love. Imagine that."

She smiled, the not-so-subtle message heard loud and clear.

"And for a baby that he wants," she added.

"And to be close to family," Jace said. "Bitsy and Sonny, not to mention Angie and Brooke, right?"

Noelle looked at her phone, reading the last text. "Maybe. Angie is currently tearing the cabin upside down and inside out again, determined to find a secret hiding place for the deed. Apparently, Garrett Delacorte was extremely *not* nice." She gave a dry laugh. "Angie used words that I don't often hear her say to describe the man."

"If she finds the deed—even if she doesn't—you can add her to the long list of loved ones living in Asheville and the surrounding area." He gave her a sly smile. "Did you happen to notice that I included myself as a loved one?"

She reached for his hand, threading their fingers. "Oh, I noticed, Dr. Fleming."

"Shhh. Don't jinx it."

"Jinx what?"

"Cassie and I have a joke that as soon as we mention my being a vet when we're out doing something fun, an emergency call comes in. So we never jinx it."

That made her laugh. "I love that kid," she said on a sigh.

"See? There's that word again. And this time, for my very own daughter."

She didn't say anything, deeply aware that he'd said he loved her on Christmas Eve and said it again the day after Christmas. It was days later, and she still hadn't said the same words to him. He didn't press; Jace wasn't pushy in that regard.

But she sensed it hurt him and that he hoped she was at least *falling* in love with him, if not yet all the way there.

She dropped her head back, quiet and thinking.

"A little music?" he asked, picking up his phone from the console. "I have good playlists. Country? Classical? Christmas? What's your pleasure?"

"Whatever you like. Can I see your playlists?"

He gave a self-conscious laugh and tapped one button to take her to his music before handing the phone to her. "Knock yourself out."

She clicked to his playlists, inching back in surprise at the one on top. "Uh, is this one called 'Noelle'? Is that all Christmas or..."

"It's all you."

"Me?"

He groaned and laughed. "I'm so busted but yeah. Since you came back, I started a short list of songs that remind me of you, past and present."

"Really?" She couldn't lie—that gave her an unexpected thrill. "That is..."

"Cheesy and romantic," he finished for her.

"And possibly the nicest thing any man has ever done for me."

"Oh, come on. You must have to fend them off left and right. I'm sure the grand gestures of rich art collectors put my little playlist to shame."

"I don't date rich art collectors," she told him. "I honestly don't date at all."

"Why not?"

She eyed him. "You didn't."

"Because I was mourning my wife and raising a young daughter. What's your excuse?"

She almost answered but the truth—whatever it was—simply didn't rise to the surface. She stared out the window, watching the snow pile along the side of the highway and flurries whiz by.

She looked back down at his phone in her hand,

thumbing through the songs. "I really don't know why," she finally said.

"Oh, you know. You just don't want to—"

"Wait. *Whoa*. Celine Dion?" She choked and sat up straight, blinking at the list. "'My Heart Will Go On'? You have the *Titanic* song on your 'Noelle' playlist?" She could barely get out the words as laughter bubbled up. "No!"

"I told you, cheesy and romantic."

"But Jace! That's next-level cheese and romance. I mean, that's brie and wine and long walks on the beach. That's—"

"I got it." He cracked up, holding up his hand to stop the onslaught. "I wish I could tell you it's one of Cassie's favorites, but she said it sounds like a sheep bleating while it's being shorn."

Noelle threw her head back and belly laughed. "She's not wrong."

"Well, it was a big hit...around that time when I knew you. And back then, I wasn't sure that, you know..."

"That your heart could go on?" she teased.

"I told you, I was a wreck. I loved you."

Her laughter faded at the confession. "You were fifteen," she said softly.

"I don't care," he replied. "I loved you. I knew what love was and it was...you."

"Oh." She put her hand on her chest. "Maybe we should—"

"Whoa! Watch—"

A jolt and thud rocked the whole truck. As the back end fishtailed, he whipped the wheel to save them from spinning out, hitting the brakes and sliding into the frozen gravel on the side of the highway.

Suddenly, they were very still and silent.

"Are you okay?" he asked, turning to her. "Are you hurt, Noelle? Are you—"

"I'm fine," she managed to breathe, shock dumping adrenaline through her. "Did we hit something?"

"A deer. Came out of nowhere." He flipped off his seatbelt. "Stay here."

He opened his door and checked for traffic, but the road was deserted. Dusk was falling along with the snow, limiting visibility.

Still trying to catch her breath, she watched him go to the front of the truck, bend over, and check the damage. Then he peered toward the wooded side of the road. Almost immediately, he took off toward the trees.

Zipping up her jacket, she opened her door and climbed out into the cold, peering into the snow to see Jace run a few feet, then drop to his knees beside an animal on the ground.

"Oh, no!" She followed, carefully finding her footing on the slope. "How bad is he?"

"I'm trying to figure that out. Can you get my bag from the back? I need the flashlight, maybe a painkiller."

She shot back to the truck and hoisted the leather bag she'd seen him take to animal patients in the past, her heart pounding against her ribs.

Please don't die, deer. Please don't die.

At least the poor baby was hit by a large animal vet, she thought as she made her way back down to him and the animal. That gave the deer a fighting chance.

"Definitely a broken leg," he said.

"What can you do?"

"Depends. I think..." He eased the animal, which seemed frozen in shock more than pain, to its back. "If it's a compound fracture and the bone is through the skin? She'll get an infection and her days are numbered unless I can get her into surgery."

Noelle groaned.

"If it's not sticking through the skin, then she's got a chance. I can't find the bone, but I don't want to hurt her." He gently felt all over the deer's leg. "We could splint it, and it might calcify and heal. Or we might have to amputate."

"Amputate? Out here?"

He didn't answer as he opened the bag and instantly found a syringe. "First, let's help her with the pain." He administered the shot, with his always-tender hands and low, comforting voice. "Now, can you get your phone and search for a vet nearby? Preferably an animal hospital open twenty-four hours. If we can get this girl to one and they'll let me work on her, well..." He patted the deer's side. "She might make it after all. Might be a three-legged deer, but they can live long and happy lives."

With a whimper, she headed back to the truck, snagged her phone, and started searching, leaving the door open so she could hear Jace. The icy air blew over her and the snow flurries fluttered into the truck, but she had to help the deer. *Had* to.

"I found one!" she called to him. "But it's thirty miles from here, in Shelby."

"We can get her there. She can make it, but I have to operate. Call them, please."

Before she could dial, she peered into the waning light to see him pick the animal up and hoist her over his shoulders, carrying her like a shepherd with a lost lamb, both hands gently protecting the broken leg.

She stared at him, frozen and not just from the air. She was...speechless. In awe and in shock and a little, well, in love.

Why couldn't she just tell him that?

Not now, she chided herself, looking down at her phone and pressing the call button. Now they had to save Doe, a deer.

NOELLE SPENT as much time peering into the truck bed as she did watching the snow accumulate in drifts on the sides of the road as they drove to the animal hospital. He'd wrapped Doe a Deer in a blanket, sedated her well, and took off.

They didn't talk, both of them concentrating on the task, the conditions, the challenge, and the possibility of losing that deer. Every once in a while, Jace reached over and took her hand, silently reassuring her that all would be well.

When he did that, she felt a million miles away from New York and the life she'd left behind. And she liked it. Heck, she kind of loved it.

When they pulled up to the well-lit entrance of the animal hospital, the automatic doors opened and two vet techs came straight out with a stretcher. Jace talked to them, helped them get the deer inside, then spent a moment at the counter, showing his license.

After a brief conversation, he walked back to Noelle, who rose from a bright orange seat in the waiting room. "I'm going to handle this operation with the vet on staff. He's small animal and they need me."

She leaned into him and gave him a kiss. "Good luck."

"I don't need it," he said. "But Doe does."

He walked toward the back and left her with an older couple who had a cat in a carrier and a young man holding a Chihuahua in his arms like a baby.

The Chihuahua, named Granny, she soon learned, was a fourteen-year-old rescue who was failing. The kitty, with the unimaginative but adorable name of Whiskers, might have swallowed a small screw, according to the concerned couple.

And she told them she'd come in with a deer they'd hit on the highway.

All of them cared so much about the animals, which was another thing that made Noelle feel like she was living someone else's life. She'd never been much of an animal person—dogs were cute, cats were complicated, fish were soothing in her dentist's office.

But now she really cared. It was Cassie, she supposed, who'd given her this love for creatures. And, of course, Jace, whose tenderness and concern for animals was truly one of the most attractive things about him. Whatever the reason, Noelle wanted that deer to be okay. And Granny. And Whiskers.

While she waited, she exchanged texts with her sisters, explaining where she was. She checked on Cassie, who was with her grandparents. Granny went in for her appointment, and then Whiskers. They came and went—no screw in Whiskers and Granny looked like she'd make it through the night.

For well over an hour, Noelle sat alone then, finally, Jace came back. He wore a medical scrub top and looked...wiped.

"Is she okay?"

On a sigh of exhaustion, he sat in the chair next to her. "We had to amputate."

"Oh, Jace."

"It was actually the best thing to do." He dropped his head back and stared at the ceiling. "If we had left her to fend in the forest, she'd have died for sure. Now she will live...on three legs."

"Where? How?"

He turned to face her. "I'm thinking she'd do well with Sonny. If he doesn't want to struggle with Doe a Deer, then I got this kid who loves animals." He grinned. "We'll find her a home."

"Really?"

"Well, I'm not putting her back in the woods. I hit her and now she's my problem." He closed his eyes. "Come to think of it, Cassie will firmly believe that three-legged deer is her personal project."

"She will," Noelle agreed with a happy sigh. "I had no idea deer could function on three legs."

"Hundred percent. We saved her life."

"You did, Dr. Fleming. Oh, whoops." She put her hand over her mouth. "Did I jinx it?"

"I can't handle any more emergencies. They said I can leave with Doe, but she's still sedated and needs to be watched. We could go home and I could come back tomorrow, but the snow is piling up. I say we hunker down here in this lovely waiting room, and we can get her home when they release her and the snowplows have been out."

She smiled at him. "Another amazing middle-of-the-night date with my favorite large animal vet."

Laughing, he pulled her into him for a kiss. "That's life on the farm, baby. You want it?"

She stilled at the question, knowing he was joking... or was he? It didn't matter. She felt the electricity right down to her toes.

Looking up at him, she whispered, "I want...you."

He lifted one brow and gave a quick look around the orange plastic-covered seats and the coffee table with year-old magazines. "Here? Now?"

She jabbed his chest. "I meant in general. In life."

He let out a noisy exhale. "Don't build me up for the most epic fall ever."

"I'm not," she said, sitting back to look at him. "Really, Jace, I'm not. I'm...confused. This has been a whirlwind romance—"

"Twenty-five years of whirlwind."

"I was grieving, we were separated, you were married for many years, and I haven't stepped foot on that mountain. The whirlwind has been this month. I met you for the second time on December first. Less than a month ago!"

"Oh, I know the day. I saw you on Creekside Road that day and we talked...and..."

"And Cassie came up and called you Daddy," she finished.

"You assumed I was married, of course."

On an easy laugh, she nodded. "And I thought she must be the luckiest woman in the whole world."

He sucked in a soft breath, silent, visibly stricken by that.

"But obviously, she...I didn't know..." Noelle brushed a hair off her face. "But Jenny was lucky to have been loved by you."

His expression softened, his eyes dimmed. "Thanks, Noelle. That means a lot."

"So, tell me..." She tapped his chest with her finger. "What did *you* think that day when we met each other for the second time?"

"Well..." He drew out the word, a smile lifting the corners of his mouth. "I couldn't really think for a few minutes after you said your name. I mean, it was Noelle Chambers! Right out of my stinkin' dreams."

She laughed again, touched by that. "You're sweet."

"No, ma'am. I'm serious." He shook his head a little, suddenly looking very much like that sweet Southern boy she'd had a crush on when she was fifteen. "And even prettier than I imagined." He traced her jaw with his fingertip, their gazes locked. "So when I pulled away and looked in my side-view at the girl who had made me once sing the *Titanic* song? I just shook my head and said, 'That's her, Cass. That's the one I'm gonna marry.'"

"*What?*"

"Oh, don't worry. She didn't hear me."

She stared at him. "Jace. You...said that?"

"I did." His fingertip was back on her lip. "'Cause I realized then and there that I still loved you, or at least the memory of who you'd been. Turns out, you're even better at forty than you were at fifteen. And, honey, that bar was high."

She studied him for a long time, lost in possibilities. "It just seems so impractical," she finally said. "And if there's one thing I am, it's practical."

"Impractical? What do you mean?"

"I don't live here. I don't work here. I don't know if I belong here. Until I do, I don't want to set up anyone —you or Cassie—for...What did you call it? The most epic fall. I don't want that."

He leaned back, falling against the pleather seat-back, letting that sink in. After a moment, he looked at her. "I think you have deeper reasons than not wanting to hurt me," he said. "I think there's more to this than impractical...ness. It's about fear."

"I'm not afraid of you."

"Not of me. Of *love*. You're afraid to love completely, because the last time you did..."

"My parents died," she whispered, the words swelling in her throat. "The last time I loved like that, I lost two people who meant the world to me." She finished fighting a sob, and instantly Jace's arm was around her.

"I know, baby," he said, stroking her hair. "I know what that feels like."

Yes, he did. This man loved and buried his wife, a toddler daughter in his arms. And yet, here he was, willing to try again. Willing to take the chance he wouldn't get hurt again.

"Listen to me, Noelle," he said. "I know this sounds like a cliché, but I'm here to tell you it really is better to love and lose than never love at all. It is." He hugged her tighter. "It really is."

Leaning into him, Noelle closed her eyes, which sent a tear down her cheek.

"You're right," she said. "It is fear. It's a real and crippling fear of that pain. It's why I've buried myself in work, why I've distanced myself from any possibility of love. I'm protecting myself."

He put his fingertips on her chin and turned her face toward him. "Well, I'm not. I believe what I'm saying, and I want to be all-in again. With you, Noelle Chambers. I love you."

Closing her eyes, she let the words roll over her. She reveled in them and pushed the fear away. She had to. She *had* to.

Looking into his eyes, she put a hand on his cheek. "Okay."

He laughed. "Okay? That's your—"

"Okay, I want to say something." Her voice sounded as unsteady as her heart, but she refused to give in to the fear. "Right here, right now, in the middle of the night, under fluorescent lights in an animal hospital in Shelby, North Carolina, I want to say..." She swallowed and leaned so close that her lips nearly touched his. "I love you, too."

He let out a soft sigh and he pulled her closer for a kiss. She melted into him, and everything changed. Her heart softened and her fears disappeared and her whole being felt lifted with hope and love.

"Excuse me, Dr. Fleming?"

They parted on a quick, self-conscious laugh and turned to the vet tech.

"We're going to release the deer to you now. She's doing very well. And the doctor said not to charge you, since you led the operation."

He stood slowly and reached for Noelle's hand. "Let's go home."

Home. Was that what Copper Creek Mountain was? Was that what this man represented?

It sure felt that way.

Chapter Twelve

Eve

"Oh, it's beautiful!" Eve gushed as they pulled up to a small development of brand-new homes perched on a rise with a commanding view of the mountains.

David drove through an open gate, past a wooden sign that said Plum Orchard, and followed the small flags to an open house on the left-hand side.

"This is nice," David said, parking on the street, even though there were no cars in the driveway, only a woman in a suit on the phone. "She must be the Realtor."

"I just want to walk around and not be talked into anything," Eve said.

"We might have to listen to a spiel." He turned off the car and took a moment to look around, taking in the size of the lots nearby, the slope of the hill, and the beautiful white clapboard farmhouse with the perfect landscaping that screamed "model home."

"Oh, hang on," Eve said as her phone buzzed from her bag. "Maybe it's Angie and she found the deed."

"I hope so, because she was talking about lifting up floorboards when we left."

"I hope it doesn't come to that." As she pulled out the cell, she sucked in a soft breath at the screen. "It's Gabby."

"Baby here?" he asked.

"I don't know." She clicked the screen and read the text.

Gabby Colson: *Hey, Eve. I'd love to talk. I have some questions. Any chance we could meet?*

She turned the phone to David and looked expectantly for his reaction.

"Oh? Is that a yes?" he asked.

"It's not a no. Let me tell her where I am and see if she wants to meet us in town for coffee. Would you?"

"Of course," he said, and the lack of hesitation touched her. Who knew her logical husband was such a risktaker?

She texted back that she and David were at an open house at Plum Orchard and could meet in an hour. That gave them plenty of time to walk through this house, hear what the agent had to say, and drive ten minutes to downtown Hendersonville.

Tucking the phone in her pocket so she'd feel it vibrate with a response, they got out of the car and walked up the short, inclined drive.

"You can go in and look around," the woman said, gesturing toward the front door. "Flyer is on the counter and lots are still available."

"Thank you." David put his arm around Eve and

guided her toward the front door. "Not sure I want to build again. How about you?"

"I'd rather not, but we'll see." She peered inside the glass-paneled front door, catching sight of the entry and living area and gleaming ash-toned hardwood floor, all decorated like *Southern Living* magazine had been here first. "Pretty so far."

Inside, it was spacious, bright, modern, and elegant.

"It's smaller than where we live now," Eve mused after they'd walked through the four bedrooms and office, which she might use for homeschooling if she continued that route.

"So's my income," David said.

They spent a few minutes walking around, then stood on the back patio, taking in the view.

"Well, what do you think?" The Realtor came out with a flyer and a smile. "They won't last long."

"It's gorgeous," Eve said. "Are there others that are move-in ready or is building our only option?"

"It depends on if you're in a hurry or not," the woman said. "I'm Barbara Winters, by the way."

They introduced themselves, made some small-talk, and headed back inside to get warm and talk in more detail.

After a few minutes and lots of questions, Eve drifted away, wanting to see the main bedroom again, imagining life in a house like this. On the way, she paused at the smallest of the other bedrooms, which would be perfect for—

"Someone else is here," David said, joining her.

"There's no wiggle room on price, but I think we could do this rather easily. The builder is solid, and the timing might work. She'll have a comparable four-bedroom ready in the spring, but of course, they need a down payment. I was getting a lot of information, but another client showed up and I didn't want to discuss financials."

"I'd put a baby girl in this room," Eve said, making him laugh. "What? I would. It's close to our room, so we could get her in the middle of the night if she cries."

"I'm laughing because you're so not thinking about builders and financials. You've got baby fever, Eve Gallagher."

She smiled. "If I do, you gave it to me."

"And Gabby made it worse."

"Or better," she corrected, sighing as she crossed her arms, looking around. "We could put a crib right there, maybe with her name on the wall. And here, by the window, a rocking chair so we could put her back to sleep in the middle of the night."

"Oh, those nights again," David said on a laugh.

"I loved those nights," Eve admitted.

"The sleepless ones? When Sawyer screamed like a banshee and it woke up Bradley, who ended up wanting to be in our bed?"

She laughed. "Yes, those nights. The challenging nights. The nights where you know why you're a parent, because a baby so tiny and helpless needs you to get them food, a clean diaper, and back to sleep." She heard the wistfulness in her voice and didn't care. "The nights when it's dark and quiet and a sweet baby is resting in your arms. I'm...excited about those nights again."

"Then you're ready."

"And so am I."

They both whipped around at the sound of the voice in the hallway, and Eve gasped when she recognized it.

"Gabby?"

The young woman stepped into the bedroom, her now familiar puffer coat unable to zip up over her very large, very ready belly.

"What are you doing here?" Eve asked.

"I knew where the development was," she said, looking up at David, who seemed stunned. "You must be Dr. Gallagher."

"Oh, hi. Yes." He extended his hand, suddenly appearing far more nervous than Eve could ever remember seeing David. "Gabby, hello. I didn't know... I was talking..."

She laughed. "I should have introduced myself out there, but I didn't want to interrupt." Then she turned to Eve. "And I didn't mean to surprise you, but here I am."

"It's wonderful to see you," Eve said, reaching to hug her. "I'm glad you're here. I'm...not sure...but I'm..."

Gabby smiled. "There's an elephant in the room and it's not just"—she tapped her belly—"me."

"How do you feel?" David asked her.

"Good. Tired. All of the usual stuff I guess one feels at nine months." She held his gaze, her expression warm, but curious. "Was it true what you said to that lady? You could pay cash for this house?"

David inched back, surprised. "Uh, yes. Assuming we get what we would ask for our house."

She nodded, then turned to Eve. "And you really like sitting with a baby in the middle of the night?"

"I'm weird like that," Eve said, reaching to slide her arm through Gabby's, because she could tell her friend was wildly uncomfortable. "Would you like to go somewhere to talk? Maybe get to know David?"

"I'd like to walk through this house with you," Gabby said. "It's nice and I want to know what you think of it. What you'd, you know, do with it."

"Of course," Eve said. "Let's go back out to the kitchen and start there."

The agent had taken another call outside again, Eve was happy to see, giving them the privacy they needed. David and Gabby exchanged a few awkward words, both of them visibly nervous. Like they each wanted to impress the other, which gave Eve a huge dose of high hopes.

"Well, I love this kitchen," Eve started. "We have a table that seats six for the kitchen and like to eat there together when David gets home from work."

"Which will be earlier now that I'll be taking over Dr. Robinson's practice. Not nearly as many late days in the OR."

"Do you eat all together every night?" Gabby asked.

"We try, but there is life—sports practices, games, and David's schedule," Eve said. "I like to cook, and I think it's an important time."

Gabby nodded. "And do you watch TV every night?"

"We do movie night," David said. "Not a lot of shows, but some."

Listening, Gabby walked toward the screened porch and looked out at a second deck.

"I'd probably put a better railing out there," David said quickly. "That one doesn't look too toddler safe."

Gabby smiled at him. "But you don't have a toddler."

"Gabby," he said on a quick laugh. "We don't have to dance around the subject. Eve has told me everything and I'm...well, I was skeptical at first, but I'm warming to the idea. Are you?"

She took a deep breath and exhaled. "I think I am," she admitted, rubbing her belly. "Especially listening to you and seeing a house like this." She made a sad face, angling her head. "I can't give this to my little girl," she whispered. "Maybe someday, but by the time I could afford it, she'll be much too old to have...the perfect childhood."

"Nothing's perfect," David replied. "All we can do is our best. Do we make mistakes? Daily. But we all try to remember that every decision is driven by love." He reached over and took Eve's hand. "I love this woman and I love our children. So much, in fact, that—"

"You're giving up a major job to take a family practice and reduce your hours and live here."

David inched back. "I guess Eve told you everything."

"No." She shook her head. "I just came from Dr. Robinson's office and, I hope you don't mind, but I talked to him really openly."

"I don't mind at all," David said.

Eve stepped forward. "What did he say, Gabby?"

"He said that if I want to give up my daughter for adoption, there is no better family she could be with." She swallowed, clearly emotional. "He said you are good people on every level, and that she'd be..." She put her hand on her stomach. "Well loved."

The last few words made her voice crack and Eve instantly put her arm around her. "She would be well loved," Eve said gently, sensing the storm brewing in this poor pregnant woman's heart. "But she would be well loved with you, too."

Gabby blinked up at her, tears brimming. "I know. That's what's so hard. I want to say yes, I know it's the right thing to do, but I'm scared I'll regret the decision."

"I get that," Eve said. "And I don't want you to regret anything."

"Would you consider an open adoption?" Gabby asked. "That means I can see her and she'd know I'm her birth mother."

Eve's heart hitched, uncertain how to respond.

"Of course," David said smoothly. "I know several people who have situations like that and as long as everyone is one hundred percent in agreement and supportive of the child, there's no reason our daughter couldn't know her birth mother. I trust she'll be confident in our love and doubly blessed to have yours."

Eve pressed her hand to her chest, loving the answer—and the man who gave it—with everything she had. "I agree," she whispered. "I simply hadn't thought of it before."

Gabby swiped at her tears with a self-conscious chuckle. "Sorry. I'm so hormonal that just thinking about some things makes me fall apart. It's embarrassing."

"It's perfectly normal," David said. "Progesterone is like cutting an onion. You're going to cry."

She smiled at that. "You sound like Dr. R. You'll be a great replacement for him."

"Thank you, Gabby."

"You'll be a great replacement for my non-existent husband, too."

David put a light hand on her shoulder. "No one is trying to replace anyone or anything," he said, his gentle bedside manner on full display. "We all want to give your baby girl the best possible life. And you, too."

"Oh." She whimpered on a sigh. "I guess I have to think a little more."

"Gabby," Eve said as an idea occurred to her. "Could I pick you up and bring you out to Copper Creek Mountain tomorrow night? I'd love for you to meet my family. You can have dinner at our cabin and get to know everyone. No strings, no pressure."

"Just more people for me to fall in love with."

Eve and David shared a smile.

"Yeah, a little," Eve said.

Gabby nodded. "I could do that. Assuming, you know, I haven't popped."

They finished the tour in what Eve hoped might be the baby's room. She knew full well Gabby was still uncertain, but with every passing minute, she clung to more and more hope that she might be holding a baby in the middle of the night very soon.

Chapter Thirteen

Angie

SOMETHING HAD TO HAPPEN. Something had to break. Something had to...be *found*.

Angie couldn't remember ever wanting anything so much. Yes, she wanted to stay in Asheville. Yes, she wanted to live in this mountain home and start over. But, oh, man, she wanted to put her hands on that deed and stick it to Garrett Delacorte in the worst imaginable way.

Bad enough that she'd literally torn the house apart and now stood over the attic floorboards with...

"What is this called again?" she asked Sonny, who stood watching, his expression a little mystified.

"Crowbar," he said. "To lift the most ornery and difficult things."

"Then I should use it on Garrett Delacorte."

Behind her, she heard Brooke snicker. "She's taking it personally," her daughter whispered. "And I'm here for it."

"How else can I take it, Brooke? That...man. That... evil, awful..."

"You can curse, Aunt Angie," Sawyer said, standing off to the side. "You've already called him some pretty bad words."

She raised her head to look at her youngest nephew, fighting a smile. "Don't you have a bear to find?"

"And miss this?" he countered, hugging the stuffed one he rarely put down closer to his little chest. "You're going to find a secret code that leads you to the hidden compartment with a buried treasure and...and...and *jewels!*"

She snorted a laugh. "You play too many video games. But jewels would be nice."

"Tanooki knows!" He waved the old, beaten-up bear. "You're going to find the bead, Aunt Angie."

"*Deed*," she corrected, smiling at her dear nephew. "But thanks for the confidence, Soy Sauce. Now, how do I use this thing, Sonny?"

Sonny shook his head and took a few steps forward. "Well, darlin', I think you should knock on the wood first."

"For luck?" she asked, screwing her face up, because she didn't need luck, she needed the deed.

"For the sound of hollow. You know what that sounds like?"

"Garrett Delacorte's chest?"

They all laughed—the boys, Brooke, Sonny. They'd been her partners throughout all of this. Eve and David were off doing whatever they did in Hendersonville. Elizabeth had gone to town to pick up her dress. Noelle had barely come down from the cloud that carried her around after yesterday's trip to Charlotte, and had left early to help Jace with...had she said *a three-legged deer*?

Angie should know, but all she could think about was finding that deed, saving the cabin, protecting her home, and, yeah, making Garrett Delacorte eat...something she didn't want to say out loud in front of these boys.

"Where should I knock?" she asked.

Sonny got down on his hands and knees and started tapping his knuckles on the floor. "Each board, and the walls, actually. Tap a few times and listen for the difference between this..." He knocked and it sounded...like knocking. Then he crawled to the boards she'd lifted the first day she was here, the ones covering a hiding spot where everything *but* the deed had been stashed away by one of her ancestors." And this," he said, knocking again. "Hear the difference?"

"I do!" James said. "One sounds like there's nothing behind it, and one sounds kind of dead or muffled."

"Good boy," Sonny said, standing up. "You got it."

"And then what?" Angie asked.

"Don't crowbar until you find something with a hollow back."

Angie let out a soft groan. "Okay, team. Start knocking. Knock on every inch of this attic and holler for the hollow!"

The kids dispersed, knuckles out, as Angie's cellphone rang. When she saw the name on the screen, she prayed this was good news from Biltmore House and not instructions to come back and rerecord with the devil himself.

"Hello, Marjorie," she said, shouldering her way out of the low-ceilinged attic to the airier hallway. "Please tell me—"

"I found something."

Angie gasped, nearly lightheaded at the news. "What?"

"The butler's log," she said. "It's not the deed you crave, obviously, but it was recorded by the butler of the day that his footman, Garland, and the parlor maid, Angelica, would be leaving their quarters to relocate to the home they'd built—"

"It says that? That they built it?"

"Yes, it does," she confirmed. "And it says, 'the home they built on land given to them by Mr. and Mrs. Winchester.' I can give you a copy."

"Oh! Yes!" Angie thrust her hand in the air, the sense of victory strong. "I mean, it's not a deed and it doesn't supersede the title, but it's something."

"It should hold up in court."

Court. That could take *years*. And Garrett was going to level this house on New Year's Day. But it was something. Maybe she could take it to Max Lynch and beg for more time.

"Thank you, Marjorie. Are you working? Can I come by and pick it up?"

"I'll email you a photograph. If you need the original, I'll get it to you, I promise."

"Okay, thank you." When she said goodbye, Angie headed back into the attic, smiling as she heard all the knocking going on.

"Nothing so far," Brooke said to her when she poked her head in. "But don't worry, Mom. If it's here, we'll find it."

"Marjorie found something from the butler's log. It might help our case, I don't know." Angie sighed and put an arm around her daughter. "Are you sure your cute boyfriend isn't steering us in the wrong direction?"

"Mom! He's not my boyfriend, for heaven's sake. And why would he?"

"Because his dad is paying him to be a double agent? To plant seeds of doubt and make us search this house when he knows darn well there's no deed here? Maybe it's somewhere else completely and he wants us off the right track and...up here."

"You need a break, woman." Brooke put a hand on Angie's shoulder and pushed her back to the hall. "Be right back," she called to her cousins. "Keep knocking!"

Outside the attic, Angie practically collapsed, leaning against the wall then sliding to the floor. "Baby, I'm wiped out from this search," she confessed.

"I know, Mom. I've never seen you this focused or determined."

Angie turned to her, studying her daughter's extraordinary features and big brown eyes. "I want this for you."

"For us," Brooke corrected.

"For *you*. Yes, we'll both be happier here, but..."

She plucked at a thread in the hall runner. "I want to give this to you. This beautiful home and a second chance and the mountain and family and all the stuff you didn't have out there in cold, cold California."

Brooke smiled. "I really appreciate that, but I'm worried about you."

"Me? I'm fine."

"No, you aren't." Brooke scooted a little closer and looked hard at Angie. "You might lose. You know that, right?"

She nodded. Then shook her head. "We're not giving up."

"No, we're not, until we do."

Angie frowned. "What does that mean?"

"It means that sometimes other people win. You don't get the guy, you aren't in first place, you can't... find the deed."

Angie stared at her, searching her face, trying to figure out... "How did you get so smart?"

Brooke laughed. "I've been listening to you," she said. "I've watched you and learned from you."

"From me?" Angie scoffed. "I'm the worst person in the world to watch. I didn't know my husband was a cheat. My daughter was on a path to destruction, and I had no idea. Now, the single greatest thing I've ever owned—aside from you—is slipping through my wildly incompetent hands. Why would you watch me?"

"Why don't you give yourself more credit?"

Angie shrugged. "I'm losing my confidence."

"Don't make me pep-talk you," Brooke teased.

"Because if I have to tell you how awesome you are, I will."

Angie smiled, then flicked her fingers, begging for more. "Just a little, please."

"Seriously, Mom. So what if we lose this house?"

"So what?" She drew back, aghast at the words. "Does the fact that it's been in our family for a hundred years mean nothing? That it was a gift to your great-great-grandmother because she saved a child's life? That it's where we are going to live from now until you go to college?"

"We just need to be together," Brooke said. "You and me. Does it really matter where we—"

"I found it! I found it!"

At the words, shouted by Aunt Elizabeth downstairs, Angie shot to her feet. "What? You found the deed?"

"No," Elizabeth called as she trudged up the stairs, waving something. "I found the receipt from the antique store. The one where I put the secretary desk on consignment. I found the store's name and we can call and find out—"

Angie crumbled right to the floor again.

Next to her, Brooke let her head fall back so hard it hit the wall with a thud.

"What? You're not excited?" Elizabeth demanded. "We've been looking for this!"

"We've been looking for the *deed*," Angie said, reaching up to take the receipt. "But who knows? Maybe this is one step closer. Maybe they still have the desk and inside the desk is a secret compartment and inside the compartment is a key that unlocks the—"

"Mom!"

"I'm sorry, Brooke. And thank you, Aunt Elizabeth, but I'm just so darn—"

"Mom!" Brooke shouted louder, this time banging her head against the wall to make her point.

"I'll stop, Brooke, when I—"

"Angel Chambers Messina!" Brooke yelled, banging her head again and again. "Listen!"

"I am listening, Brooke, I—"

"To the wall!"

Brooke froze, and so did Angie.

"To the...what did you say?"

Slowly, Brooke turned around and lifted her fisted hand, knocking on the wall. Once. Twice. Three times. Maybe more, since the three boys and Uncle Sonny all crawled out of the attic to see what was going on.

"Knock again, Brooke," Angie said so softly, she barely heard her own voice.

She tapped again. And again.

"Hollow."

They said the word together, mother and daughter, sharing that bonded look that was strong as steel and just as lasting. Right at that moment, Angie didn't care if they got this house. She didn't even care if they stayed in Asheville.

All she cared about was the love she shared with this amazing, brilliant, beautiful young woman she'd raised. How did that happen? How had Brooke become her best friend, her confidante, her partner in crime?

Angie shook her head, yanking herself from her thoughts, blinking to see Sonny bracing the crowbar into the baseboard of the wall.

"What are you doing?" she asked, suddenly realizing what was happening.

Before he could answer, he popped the wood, then pulled at the drywall panel right above it, so thin it came out in his hand.

And behind it, a dark hole.

"What?" Brooke got on her knees to peer in, pulling out her phone to turn on the flashlight. "Oh, my..." She turned around and looked at Angie. "Do you see?"

She shifted her gaze from her beautiful daughter into the dark space in the wall, the beam of light moving straight to the back, landing on a big round dial that had to be the combination lock...*to a safe*.

She almost screamed with joy. Holy *Moses*. They'd found it.

"Knock and the door shall be opened," Elizabeth whispered once they'd all settled down, stopped cheering and high-fiving, and finally had a plan.

First of all, no one touched it. With the proper light, Sonny would use the crowbar to attempt to open the large metal box with a combination lock on the front. If that didn't work, they would contact a professional.

"A safe-cracker!" James exclaimed. "Cool."

"And if that doesn't work," Sonny added, "I have a pistol and we can crack it the old-fashioned way."

Sawyer practically danced at the idea.

With all the flashlights they could muster, Sonny headed in, holding the crowbar, muttering what Angie knew for sure was a prayer.

But hers had been answered. The deed had to be in there and she'd be waving it hard in Garrett's face, then calling moving companies to get her stuff in California. They'd enroll Brooke in the local high school here and by January—

"It's not locked."

At Sonny's words, she crawled closer, the first tendril of worry winding its way through her chest. "It's not?"

With one hand and no crowbar, he inched the metal door open, eliciting a gasp from all of them, the loudest from Angie.

"You look, Ange," Sonny said, holding up a powerful flashlight.

"Okay." She inched her head around the door, blinked into the metal box and saw...a paperclip. And a button. And a broken piece of porcelain.

Seriously?

"There's nothing in here."

At the collective groan, she reached up and took the flashlight, shining it first on the round metal button, and then... "Wait! What's that? Something lodged behind the back!"

She reached in gingerly, spying the corner of a white piece of paper slid deep in the recesses of the safe.

"Is it a false wall, Mom?" Brooke asked. "Sometimes they have those to really fool the bad guys."

"Let me...get this." Using her fingernails, she pried the paper out, hoping against hope that deeds were very thin back in the day. Because this one was not very substantial. "I almost have it. I almost have it!"

"Come on, Angie!" A few of them clapped and it felt like everyone drew closer.

"Got it!" She eased the folded paper out and dropped onto her backside with a sigh of success.

"What's it say?"

"Open it!"

She looked down at the white paper and fought the disappointment starting to strangle her. There was no way this was a deed.

Very slowly, she unfolded it and read the hand-written words.

Jane Benson's Peach Cobbler

No! She wanted to scream.

"Cobbler?" Sonny asked, reading over her shoulder.

"Oh, Granny Jane's cobbler was to die for," Elizabeth said softly. "I've always wanted that recipe."

Angie couldn't even muster a harsh look or a quick laugh. Peach Cobbler?

"Maybe it's code," Bradley suggested.

"Or that back is false," Brooke added.

"You look," Angie said to Sonny, too devastated to continue.

"I will." Kneeling, he reached in, snagged the button, and handed it to Angie, then placed the broken porcelain on the floor.

Fighting tears, Angie curled her fingers around the ornate metal button, squeezing so hard it dug into her palm. This was not a deed. That recipe was not a deed. Nothing was a deed.

While Sonny worked on the back of the safe, she made her way to Brooke, who put a loving arm around her.

"Don't give up yet, Mom."

"I still have the antique receipt," Elizabeth reminded her. "That deed could be stuck in some secret compartment—"

"No, it's not," she said glumly. "This was just too good to be true."

"The safe?" Elizabeth asked.

"The whole idea. Moving here. Living here. Starting over and..." Her voice caught as she lost the battle not to cry.

"There's no false back," Sonny said, sounding as sad as she felt. "What you see is what you get on this safe."

Angie dropped her head back and let out a sorrowful moan, which just made them all gather around to comfort her.

"Come on, dearest darling," Elizabeth said, taking

her hand. "You could go to the antique store in Black Mountain."

"Or I could give up and let Garrett Delacorte win."

Elizabeth sighed. "Hating him is only hurting you, Ange. The best thing to do is to forgive him."

"Forgive him?" she scoffed, knowing she was a long, long way from that.

"Then you start to look for the next path, and it will be clear," Elizabeth continued. "You and Brooke can live at Sonny's farm with us for a bit, until you figure it out. I think I'm going to be very happy there after we're married."

Married. Squeezing her aunt's hand, Angie realized that she'd barely done a thing for the wedding that was happening in two days. She'd been so wrapped up in this fruitless search, she'd let everyone else do the work and that was wrong on every level.

"We'll see," she said, forcing herself up.

"Do you want the antique receipt? The address is on there."

"What I want," she said slowly, knowing they all expected her to say "is the deed." But she clung to her aunt's hand and looked into her eyes. "Is to help you with the place cards that need to be written, to check on the barn and string more lights, and get ready for the happiest day of your life."

Elizabeth smiled and stood with her. "And I appreciate that, but the boys will do that work. You are going to go to the antique store for one last shot."

She huffed a sigh. "Is it worth it?"

"We have two more days. It's worth it. Eve has invited her new friend for dinner. Who knows? We may have reason to celebrate. Trust the Lord, dearest darling."

She already knew the antique store was a dead end. But what was one more at this point?

Chapter Fourteen

Noelle

JACE PLACED Doe in her own special stall at his place, and Noelle could already tell the deer would be able to survive on three legs. Cassie, no surprise, was over the moon about the new arrival.

"I think we can just keep her here forever," Cassie said as they all climbed into Jace's truck for a trip to town to retrieve the repaired locket. "We have the room."

"Not if we get too many sick animals that need to board," Jace said. "Sonny said he'd love to take her, and he has the space to keep her separate from the sheep until she's strong and used to his farm."

"And you go there all the time," Noelle reminded Cassie, turning to see if she'd latched her seatbelt in the booster seat. "So you can see Doe whenever you want."

"But what about you, Miss Noelle? When will you see her?"

"Her middle name should be 'Relentless,'" Jace joked as he turned on the engine.

Noelle laughed. "When I come to visit, which I told you will be very frequently."

Cassie looked a little dubious, and asked permission to play *Animal Crossing* on her iPad, something she rarely did in the truck. She liked to talk—more than almost anyone Noelle had ever met—so she sensed something wasn't quite right when Cassie asked for the distraction.

"Sure," Jace said, apparently not concerned. "Can you reach behind my seat and get it for her?"

Noelle did, but before she handed the iPad to Cassie, she made direct eye contact with the child, trying to gauge her mood.

"Everything okay with you, Cass?"

She nodded, but her big gray-blue eyes looked troubled.

"You nervous about being a flower girl?"

This time she shook her head, still uncharacteristically quiet.

"About Doe the Deer?"

"She'll be okay," she said softly, reaching for the iPad. "Can I?"

Noelle relinquished it and turned around, glancing at Jace to see if he'd followed the whole interaction or shared any of her concerns.

"She can count days, you know," he whispered.

The comment just made Noelle sigh as she followed what he was saying. Cassie, like Jace and Noelle, knew darn well that their time together would end the day after the wedding.

New year, old life.

The words echoed in her head, along with others she'd spoken last night. She'd told Jace she loved him, and never meant anything more.

As if he understood what she was thinking about, he reached over the console and took her hand, holding it for the whole drive to downtown, all three of them quiet and...counting days.

They parked, walked together to the jewelry store, and peeked into store windows, but for the most part, all three of them were off today. Was it the late, late night with the deer? The looming goodbye? Noelle knew that something had this little not-quite-a-family seeming different today.

As they walked into the jewelry store, Noelle replayed that thought. They weren't quite a family, but somehow the three of them had bonded. They had inside jokes. They'd shared many meals, experiences, hugs, and, well, life. Only for the past month, but it had been intense and Noelle was so reluctant to give it up.

The jeweler waved to her from his table in the back, and Noelle headed there, leaving Jace and Cassie to wait and wander around the glittery cases.

"You left the locket, as I recall," the man said, pulling open a long drawer. "I have it right here."

With the necklace dangling, he stood to come closer, laying the gold chain and locket on a velvet pad in front of her.

"It's good as new," he said, demonstrating how the

hinge worked. "You can replace these old pictures now with your husband and daughter's."

"Oh, they're..." She froze for a minute, realizing how much she didn't want to deny that's what Jace and Cassie were. No, they were not her husband and daughter, but right then—just like last night and for the last half hour in the car and pretty much every day since she'd laid eyes on both of them—she *wanted* them to be.

"Thank you," she finished instead, taking the necklace. "This actually belongs to someone else, and my aunt is wearing it in her wedding."

"Oh, you told me that." The man chuckled, tapping his temple as if his brain had let him down. "Sorry. I'm old and don't have the gray matter I used to."

"Well, it certainly hasn't affected your work," Noelle said as she gestured toward the repaired necklace. "This is perfect."

After paying him, she joined Jace and Cassie, who, instead of kidding around about tiaras and diamond rings like last time, were both waiting on seats in the front. Cassie had her face in the iPad she'd brought, which didn't sit well with Noelle.

In fact, it made her heart ache.

Noelle didn't say anything as they walked out and turned left to head back to the car, but she stopped, looking around at where they were. She didn't know every street corner in the quaint downtown, but she recognized this one. The Red Bus wasn't far, and neither was...something else.

"Hey, can we go this way?" she said, pointing to the side street. "I saw something when I was in town before Christmas, and I want to check it out."

"Sure." Jace gave Cassie a tug and they followed Noelle, whose heart rate increased with every step. Suddenly, she really, really wanted to get to her destination and see one thing still in the window of Spruce Studio Art.

Gallery For Sale or Lease

She took in a quick breath when she saw the sign, making Jace slow his step.

"You like that?" he asked, assuming her response was to the gorgeous abstract displayed above the sign.

Not quite sure what to say, she nodded. "Mind if we go in?"

"Of course not." He looked down at Cassie, who seemed even less enthralled with this errand than the last. "Don't touch anything, Cass."

"I won't."

Noelle led the way into the gallery, instantly loving the very scent of the place. An art gallery had always been like home to her, having interned in several of them and worked in a small studio in Soho before getting her job with Sotheby's.

She loved the soothing vibe of most galleries, and this one was no different. Small and personal, it featured some local artists and some bigger names. She paused at one massive black and gold oil painting that somehow had both hard edges and soft sides.

"Beautiful, isn't it?" A woman in a dark dress with a

gorgeous mane of braided hair came to stand next to her, following Noelle's gaze. "It's a Tappan. John Tappan. He lives over in Tennessee and—"

"Oh, I recognize a Tappan," she said. "I adored his 'Woods' series." She'd also sold two of them to collectors in Upstate New York. "But this gold is a step out for him."

She was aware of Jace on one side of her, observing the conversation, and the intense gaze of the woman, who probably didn't meet a lot of people who knew the artist John Tappan.

"I'm Sherry Kinsell," the woman said. "I own this gallery. You're a collector?"

"Not exactly." Noelle shook her hand and introduced herself and Jace. Cassie had found a seat—or Jace had guided her to it—and she was back on her electronic device playing a game.

"How long have you owned the gallery?" Noelle asked, biting back a million other questions that were aching to get out.

"Actually, it belonged to my husband, Zander."

"Zander Kinsell? Oh, of course. I didn't recognize your last name."

"You knew him?" she asked, brows rising.

"I did a few deals with him," Noelle said. "I work at Sotheby's in New York. I'm a director of luxury art and I believe Zander was the man who helped me nail my first Stephan Braun etching."

"Oh, my goodness!" Sherry clapped her hands. "I remember when he sold that."

"To my client." Noelle frowned. "And Zander is..."

"He passed away about a year ago," she said on a sigh.

Noelle pressed her hand to her chest, immediately picturing the exuberant dealer who was quite a talented painter in his own right. "What a terrible loss," she murmured. "I'm so sorry."

"You have my deepest condolences," Jace added warmly.

"Thank you. It was sudden—a heart attack. I've tried so hard to keep this gallery, which he opened thirty-four years ago. But I'm in over my head and, well..."

"You're selling it," Noelle said.

"Or I'd lease it," Sherry told her. "But even in a town that loves art like this one, there aren't many people who are qualified to know good art and how to buy and sell..." Her voice faded as she eyed Noelle. "Do you know anyone?"

"I might." She took a deep breath, wildly aware that Jace was listening to every word and she hadn't even talked to him about it, but... *Here goes nothing.* "I'm interested."

The woman gasped softly, but next to her, she felt Jace take a full step backwards as the impact of what she'd just said hit him.

"You are?" They both asked the question at precisely the same time.

Noelle gave a soft laugh and looked from one to the other, holding Jace's surprised and delighted gaze a second or two longer. "At least, I'd like to talk about it."

"Let's talk!" Sherry said excitedly. "Would you like to look around? Then, if you want, we can chat or you can come back without your family. Whatever you like."

Once again, she didn't correct the mistake. It felt too good. And so did standing in this art gallery seriously considering changing her whole life.

The door dinged with two new customers and Noelle gestured toward them. "You go and sell, Sherry. Can we just look around?"

"All you want," she said, her ebony eyes dancing with excitement.

When she stepped away, Noelle finally let out her breath.

"Uh..." Jace leaned in. "This is my shocked face."

She smiled. "I'm not committing to anything—"

"Only buying a business in Asheville."

She held up her hand. "Considering it. I first saw the sign when I was Christmas shopping. Elizabeth planted the seed, of course, but last night, at the animal hospital..."

"The seed got watered," he finished, reaching for her hand. "Noelle. This is huge."

"Too much? Too soon?"

"Are you crazy? You know how I feel about you," he said, both of them keeping their voices barely above a whisper. "Would this be the right move for you?"

She thought about that for a moment, walking from

the painting she'd been admiring to a wall of watercolors, all seascapes but extremely well done, with attention to detail, glorious colors, and a strong artistic "voice" that managed to convey a range of emotions, from awe to fear to utter contentment.

Or maybe she was just taking a reading of her heart.

"I love the size of this place and the feel," she said, turning to take in how elegant the displays were, and how perfectly spaced.

"I have to ask you something," he said, getting closer. "Because I really don't know your business, but would buying or leasing a gallery be a step down from your lofty position at a company with the international name recognition that Sotheby's has?"

She crossed her arms, staring at an iron sculpture on a tower display, but not really seeing the art.

"The key word there is 'international,'" she told him. "My dream has always been to run my division in the London office. Probably since Aunt Elizabeth took us there a few years after my parents passed. I fell in love with the city, and every trip I've taken since only made me love it more."

"But this promotion you're up for next month—that's not the London job you want."

She shook her head. "It was a stepping stone, putting London a year or two away."

"Was?" he asked. "Does this have to do with the management changes your boss mentioned?"

"If Lucinda takes the recently-opened slot in

London, then she could stay for ten years or more. I would have to wait my turn and I'd be fifty." She made a face. "Hard as that is to swallow."

"And if she doesn't take it?"

She shrugged. "Depends on who gets it. I knew Nigel, the man who held the job, wasn't going to stay forever. I was hoping he'd stick around for a year or two, then I could..." She shook her head and stopped. "That's not why I'd do this, Jace. This isn't about London and my dream of living there. This is about..."

"Us," he finished, taking both her hands.

"Our future. Maybe soon, maybe later. Cassie looks worried, you look sad, and I..." She managed a smile. "Like I mentioned last night—I am a woman in love."

His eyes shuttered as he pulled her closer, hugging her. She looked over his shoulder to take in the perfect light, quality art, and beautiful surroundings, but instead her gaze fell on Cassie. She'd abandoned the iPad and turned on the chair to stare out the window.

For all her bravado and personality, Cassie was scared, too.

"I love her, too," she whispered to Jace.

He drew back, glancing at Cassie, then back at Noelle. "She's irresistible, I know. But, babe, you can't make life decisions and buy businesses and walk away from London dreams because your heart got stolen by the world's greatest kid. She will be a teenager some-day, you know. You might not love her so much then."

"It's not just her and you know it." She pressed her hand to his cheek. "Dad's pretty irresistible, too, you know. And, by the way, I knew a teenage Fleming and he was..." Her throat swelled. "As perfect as he is now."

He smiled, his own eyes misty. "And you're sure this isn't just because London has slipped out of your hands?"

"Jace." The comment hurt a little, but she respected that he had to be sure. That she had to know exactly what she was doing and why.

"Okay now." Sherry came hustling back over, still smiling. "Would you like to talk seriously? My one and only salesperson is on her way back from lunch and we could go in the office."

"Well, I..."

"Yes," Jace said. "You two talk. I'll take Cassie for some ice cream and a trip to the toy store. Then I'll swing back and get you."

She nodded, knowing that everything was getting...real.

AN HOUR LATER, Noelle knew that leasing the art gallery with an option to buy was eminently doable. She could rent from Sherry, who was happy to stay on as the manager, for as long as Noelle liked. Then, once Noelle decided to leave Sotheby's completely, she could sell her apartment in New York and use the profit to buy the gallery outright.

So it might be long distance for a while. Then, there was a plan for moving from that to...this.

It was a change, but a gradual one that made sense and seemed more natural than throwing her life and career to the four winds and moving here.

The thought rocked her as she pulled open the door and stepped into the chilly winter air. Jace had texted that he and Cassie were on their way from the toy store, so she started off in that direction to meet them.

As she walked down the street and looked in the windows of the quaint boutiques and funky restaurants of Asheville, she compared it to New York City...or London.

She could be done with New York, no doubt about it. After all these years, she was ready to end her days in the Big Apple and start over somewhere else. She'd always imagined that would be in England, with a darling flat near Berkeley Square and maybe friends with a house in the country for long weekends.

She pictured herself walking under that famous navy awning on New Bond Street, part of the Sotheby's London team, the best of the best in the international art world. She'd lunch with clients at The Savoy and shop on Oxford Street.

That was the "next phase" of life she'd been planning on during the twenty years she'd conquered New York.

But now...there was Jace. And, yes, Cassie. And her sisters and aunt and Asheville, North Carolina. Was this where she belonged? Was this the right home for

Noelle Chambers, who thrived on the noise, traffic, and bustle of the big city?

Home is where the heart is, right?

"Miss Noelle!"

Noelle looked up at the sound of the familiar high-pitched voice, laughing when she saw Cassie running toward her holding a sizeable stuffed animal.

"Look! I got a deer! It can be friends with Doe while she recovers!"

Jace laughed, rolling his eyes. "Blame the after-Christmas sale."

"This deer is beautiful," Noelle said, taking the stuffed animal that Cassie proudly held out. "Doe will love it."

"Daddy said it can be like an emo...emotion..." She looked up at him, confused.

"Emotional support animal," he supplied. "We all could use those once in a while. So, how did it go back there?"

"Did you buy a picture, Miss Noelle? Daddy said you were buying something."

"I didn't buy anything...yet." She took both their hands and pulled them closer, suddenly overwhelmed with how much she loved them both. "Now, shouldn't we get home to Doe and see how she's doing?"

"Yes!" Cassie pranced ahead, holding her deer.

But Jace held back for a second, lifting a brow. "Did you say...home?"

She sighed. "I guess I did."

Chapter Fifteen

Eve

"How do I preheat this thing?" Eve stared at the unfamiliar oven dials, her mind whirring, her heart racing, and her whole body tense with nerves. Would her prized meatloaf—literally no one didn't love her meatloaf—take the same forty-seven and a half minutes in this oven as it did at home?

She turned, suddenly remembering the table. Should she set it now? Oh, wait, James did that. "I'm not sure about those turquoise placemats, though," she muttered, walking toward the farmhouse table, wondering if they should go for something more subdued.

"Oh, wait. Did Bradley get the sparkling water from the garage fridge?" She spun again, looking around, catching sight of the clock. "And no way it's that late. Where are Angie and Brooke? And Noelle?"

On her next turn, her gaze landed on Aunt Elizabeth, who sat perched at the island, sipping her late afternoon tea, watching Eve, her expression amused.

"My goodness, you're a nervous wreck over one dinner guest."

Eve puffed out a breath, recognizing that her need for control was out in full force. "Well, David's on his way with Gabby after he met with Dr. Robinson and...and..."

She shook off her nerves and stared at her aunt, the truth about why she was having Gabby for dinner bubbling up. She managed to keep it in.

After meeting with Gabby yesterday, Eve and David had decided not to tell anyone that an adoption was under consideration. They agreed it was entirely up to Gabby to share how, with whom, when...and, of course, if at all.

He'd gone down to Hendersonville for another meeting with Terrance Robinson, and planned to pick up Gabby to bring her here. They'd talk about all that timing in the car, Eve knew.

Her family probably thought it was strange that Eve wanted to have her new friend for dinner two days before the wedding, but time was running out. Gabby could go into labor any day and Eve wanted her to meet the family, and deliver the baby knowing her final decision on adoption.

"But they need to be here to meet her," Eve said, half to herself as she realized how very important it was that Gabby know her boys, her sisters, and her aunt.

Elizabeth took a tiny sip of tea, then set the cup down. "Noelle has been with Jace and Cassie all day and, based on the last text she sent, she's, uh, shopping."

"Shopping?" Eve asked, exasperated. "Christmas is over, she has all the 'somethings' for the wedding. What is she shopping for?"

Laughing lightly, Elizabeth said, "I'll let her tell you."

"What about Angie and Brooke? Didn't you say they went to the antique store a long time ago?"

"They did." Elizabeth's smile disappeared. "And they have hit brick wall after brick wall. There was one last wild goose to chase when the antique dealer thought she knew who bought the desk, and that sent them up north to Mars Hill but—"

"*Mars Hill*? When are they getting back?"

Elizabeth slid off the stool and came around the counter, arms out. "Eve, why is this so important?"

She swallowed, tamping down the truth. "It...just is." She searched her aunt's face, longing to trust her, knowing she could trust her but— "Oh! Is that a car in the driveway? Is it David? Is it Gabby?"

She shot toward the living room and the front door.

"I'll just preheat the oven for you," Elizabeth said on a laugh that Eve barely heard.

"It's Angie and Brooke!" she exclaimed, opening the door to usher them in faster. "And they have Noelle!"

She walked into the cold, aching to bring them all in faster before Gabby got here. She slowed her step as they all got out of the SUV and processed the range of emotions on their faces.

Elizabeth joined her, walking toward Angie and Brooke first. "I take it you had no luck?"

"I'm sorry, you guys," Angie said in a reed-thin voice. "Nothing, nada, zero, zilch."

"We went into town to meet with the lawyer, Max, for one last shot," Brooke said. "He was really nice but..."

"But his client is the devil incarnate," Angie said. "And we're losing this entire property on January first. He threw money at people to get it torn down on New Year's Day! How despicable is he?"

"Beyond," Eve agreed, putting aside her stress to hug her sister. "But we can figure something out, Ange. I promise."

"When we left the lawyer, we ran smack into Noelle and Jace and Cassie in town," Brooke said, trying so hard to lighten the mood.

"And I came home with them," Noelle added, "because we got your, um, six—"

"Seven," Angie corrected.

"—texts demanding we be here for dinner," Noelle finished. "You look unhinged, Eve. And Angie is broken. Am I the only happy triplet?"

"Unhinged isn't unhappy," Elizabeth said, putting her hand on Eve's back.

"What has you so happy, Noelle?" Eve asked, determined to put aside her issues and give her sisters the love and attention they deserved.

"Nothing major. I'm just seriously considering giving up my life and career, leasing an art gallery in Asheville with an option to buy, and, you know, planning the rest of my life with the guy I've adored since I was fifteen." She grinned. "What has *you* unhinged?"

Eve felt her jaw drop and a laugh bubble up. "That's amazing, Noelle."

"It is," Elizabeth agreed. "But you're going to lease and keep Sherry Kinsell as the manager? That's a bit... halfway, don't you think? Why don't you just bite the bullet, buy the place, and...I need another B word."

"Betroth," Brooke quipped. "Is that a word?"

"It's..." Noelle's eyes shuttered. "Change. And I admit, I don't make those real big and real fast. Eve, what is so important about tonight?"

"It just is," Elizabeth answered for her, putting an arm around Eve. "She's very excited about our guest and all we can do in this moment is respect that and be here for Eve."

Eve glanced at her aunt, wondering, *Does she know?* Was that possible? Maybe this was the time to tell them, standing right out here in the waning winter light and cool breeze with the women she loved most in the whole world. Would David understand if—

The rumble of David's car coming from Creekside Road stopped her. If Gabby wanted them to know, she reminded herself, she'd tell them tonight. It simply wasn't Eve's place to make any announcements.

She smiled at them, and reached for her sisters' hands. "Noelle, I am so thrilled that you're even considering this change. And Ange." Eve drew her closer. "At the risk of sounding exactly like Aunt Elizabeth, maybe it's time to let go and let God, as the Bible says."

"That's not *exactly* in the Bible," Elizabeth corrected her. "But the idea of trusting the Lord is on every page. So I fully agree, dearest darlings. God has a plan and if His plan is to take this cabin and property away from us, it's because there's something better."

Angie's shoulders dropped with a deep sigh of disappointment. "Okay. Whatever. I'm done searching. But, Noelle's right. Why are you unhinged, Eve? What is so important about this girl?"

Eve looked over Angie's shoulder as David's sedan pulled in. "I'll let her tell you."

GABBY DIDN'T MAKE any major announcements over dinner, but she was friendly, interested in everyone, and looked to be almost as nervous as Eve. She shifted uneasily in her seat a few times, and barely ate a bite, though she raved about the meatloaf.

The grandmother who'd raised the girl must have taught her fine table manners, Eve decided. Gabby used her napkin, didn't interrupt people, and even kept her elbows off the table—a point of old-school etiquette that Eve had all but abandoned trying to teach her boys.

But, whoa, she seemed young. Even though she was

four years older than Brooke, she seemed far less worldly and shy next to the vivacious teenager. In fact, Gabby connected best with Eve's boys, talking video games and promising Sawyer that he would, if he stuck around long enough, spot himself a bear.

Far too young to have a baby...*right*?

Gabby was enthralled by Noelle's story about the deer, properly sympathetic about the missing deed, and...very quiet about her baby. Although they'd all congratulated her, no one at the table was bold enough to ask personal questions, so maybe that was why she stayed completely off the topic.

As dinner ended, Eve glanced at David, who had surreptitiously studied the young woman with the same interest Eve had. He was just as worried as Eve about Gabby's final decision.

"So, I understand there's a big wedding about to happen," Gabby said, smiling at Elizabeth. "Eve told me it's your first?"

Elizabeth laughed. "At sixty-three, if you can believe that."

"I'm surprised you're so cool about it."

"Just about everything is done, thanks to my lovely wedding planners." She gestured around the table. "And I do hope you get to meet Sonny. He's with the new deer tonight, but said he'll be over for dessert."

"There actually is one more fairly big wedding job to do," Noelle said as the boys started picking up dishes and taking them into the kitchen. "We have to wrap the wedding favors. If you add your hands to the mix, Gabby, we'll be done in no time."

"I'd love that," she said brightly, pushing back, but wincing as she did.

"Are you okay?" Eve asked.

"I'm good. Ready to roll, I guess." She patted her belly as she stood. "She's been dancing all day."

Leaving the boys and David to supervise the cleanup, Eve guided Gabby toward the sunroom, where that morning, Noelle had set up another well-managed assembly line.

"How are your ribbon-tying skills, Gabby?" Noelle asked, pointing toward the Hershey's Kisses that would go in white mesh bags, tied with ribbon and a little heart that said, "Midnight Kisses from the new Mr. and Mrs."

"No!" Gabby lifted one of the favors.

"No, you can't tie, or, no, you can't believe how cliché that is?" Elizabeth asked on a laugh. "It was my idea, so I'll take the blame."

"Take the credit," Gabby said. "I meant, no, I can't believe how utterly adorable this is." She sat on the sofa next to Eve, stifling a grunt as she lowered her very pregnant body.

Eve flinched in sympathy, vividly remembering the last few days of her own pregnancies.

"My ribbons will be crooked, and I might eat a favor or two," Gabby said, and she suddenly looked a little...overwhelmed.

"I know," Eve said. "We're a lot."

"No, actually, y'all are perfect."

Eve wanted to cheer that comment—they *were* perfect—but there was a deep sadness to Gabby's voice that made her uneasy.

"Are you sure you want to do this?" Eve asked.

Gabby looked up at her. "By this, do you mean make wedding favors or..." She put her hand on her belly and mouthed, "The other thing."

Eve's heart dropped but Angie snorted a laugh. "If the other thing is 'have a baby,'" she said with a tease in her voice, "I don't think you have much of a choice. She's coming out, whether you want her to or not." She pointed at Brooke. "And it will be a wild and wonderful ride."

"*If* I keep her." She spoke the words so softly, Eve wasn't sure she'd heard right. But by the reaction in the room, she guessed she had.

"If you..." Brooke broke the shocked silence. "Are you considering *adoption*, Gabby?"

Every cell in Eve's body stilled as she waited for Gabby to answer.

"I am considering it," she said slowly, her gaze moving to meet Eve's.

Considering. It was all Eve heard. And, no surprise, the others shared looks, leaned forward, and suddenly put two and two together and came up with...

"You haven't told them, Eve?" Gabby asked.

"Adoption is your decision, Gabby. And your announcement to make, not mine."

Angie gasped and put both hands over her mouth.

Noelle dropped a bag of Hershey's Kisses.

Brooke choked in shock.

Aunt Elizabeth just smiled and put her hand on Gabby's thigh. "That would be the most glorious thing I've ever heard. You know, God never fails to astound me with His gifts and grace. What a beautiful, loving, blessed decision."

"Do you think so?" Gabby asked her. "Because I'm...not sure."

Not sure. Eve's heart did another drop and dip. "Well, I guess you've all figured out why Gabby's here," she said.

Gabby grinned. "Nah. I came for that meatloaf."

The joke broke the ice, making them laugh, squeal, and lean in like they were ready to fire a thousand questions.

But Gabby asked the first one. "So, what do you— the two sisters who were in the womb with this woman —think of that idea?"

Angie and Noelle shared a look, a glimmer of pride in their eyes, the way all three of them always reacted when their triplet-ness was pointed out.

"I think," Angie said, "that you are both inspiring."

"Not me," Eve scoffed. "This is the woman calling the shots."

"She is, and it's a big, bold, brave thing to do," Angie said. "But don't underestimate yourself, Evie. You're willing to take a chance and change a life and grow your family and..." She shook her head. "I'm just impressed with both of you, and beyond supportive, whatever you decide."

"Thank you." Gabby turned to Noelle and gave her an expectant look.

"I've learned something huge this month," Noelle said. "And that is that you can love a child that isn't biologically yours with the same fervor and intensity that you love one you gave birth to. I'm starting to feel that way about Cassie." Her voice caught with a sob. "And I can't wait to be an aunt again."

Eve wiped a tear that rolled over her cheekbone, gratitude for her sisters swamping every other emotion.

"I appreciate all of that," Gabby said with a long exhale. "I'm confused, I'm not going to lie."

"It's not an easy decision," Eve added. "No one expects you to make it without a lot of thought."

Gabby picked up a few Hershey's Kisses and slid them into a white mesh bag, quiet for a moment.

"It's actually a very easy decision," she finally said. "You are a loving, secure family and you, Eve? Obviously, like, the world's greatest mother."

Eve smiled. "I know three boys who might disagree when they are up to their eyeballs in schoolwork and there's a new video game out."

"But you wouldn't let them play it until the work is done," Gabby said. "Which is what makes you great."

"Don't deny it, Eve," Noelle said. "You and Angie are both amazing moms."

"And Gabby would be amazing, too," Elizabeth

said, her voice always the one of love and reason. "The question is what feels right to you, Gabby."

"Both ways feel right," Gabby said. "Giving her up for adoption by Eve and David feels...easier. Not that going to college is easy, but doing it without an infant would be. That said, I've grown this sweet angel for nine months. I've given up things I love, watched my body darn near double in size, lost so much sleep it hurts, and even had to stop working because my ankles and feet were like balloons."

"You've done more than many, many twenty-year-olds would have," Eve said. "And no matter who raises your daughter, she will know that was a gift to her."

Gabby smiled at her. "I think you're awesome, Eve. I really think that God or the universe or whatever put you in my life for a reason. But sometimes I wake up in the middle of the night because she moved and I just..." She swallowed. "I love her."

And down went the rollercoaster, leaving Eve's heart in her throat. "Of course you do."

"But maybe that's why I should say yes."

Eve stared at her, not trusting herself to say anything. She couldn't or shouldn't try to sway Gabby. This was her decision and hers alone. Her sisters, niece, and aunt obviously knew that, too, because they were very quiet.

After a moment, Gabby put down the mesh bag and picked up another piece of candy. She stared at it until Elizabeth gently leaned into her.

"You can eat that, you know. We have lots."

Gabby smiled. "I might. This baby girl loves chocolate." She started to unwrap the foil, then closed her eyes as a sob escaped.

"Oh, dearest darling." Elizabeth instantly had her arm around the girl, and they all moved closer to comfort, but not overwhelm her. "Do you have faith?"

"I used to," Gabby said. "My grandma liked to read the Bible to me."

"Did you have a favorite scripture?"

She thought about that, frowning and looking into the distance. "Yes. Something about not leaning on your own understanding."

Elizabeth beamed. "And He will make clear the path!"

The sisters and Brooke had to laugh; they'd heard that expression so many times this past month.

"I hope so, because—oh!" Gabby sat up straight, her eyes growing very wide. "Oh, my goodness!"

"Did you have a contraction?" Eve asked. "Another Braxton—"

Gabby held up both hands, trembling, shaking her head, and looking down. "I think...I think...I think my water broke!"

With a collective gasp, everyone but Gabby and Eve shot to their feet.

"This is it," Gabby said, squeezing Eve's hands. "And I'm getting a contract—" She grimaced through pain. "Please, Eve, please. Stay with me. Come to the hospital with me."

"Of course. David!" she called as she tried to stand, but Gabby clung to her.

"Don't leave me," she begged, her voice calming as the contraction passed.

"I won't. I promise. I won't." She wrapped her arms around the younger woman. "You got this, honey. You can do this."

"I still don't know what to do," she said on a sob as David rushed in.

"Well, first..." Eve carefully helped her to stand. "You're going to have a baby."

Eve took the coffee David handed her and tried to smile. But after seventeen hours spent waiting for a baby to arrive, she was out of smiles.

"Is she awake?" Eve asked. "I had to sneak out to the bathroom and just sit here for a moment. I didn't miss the baby, did I?"

David shook his head and sat beside her. "Of course not. But Terrance says she's really close. He's in the doc lounge doing some work."

"So she's alone?"

"With nurses. In and out of sleep. Everything's normal, but this little newborn doesn't seem to be in a hurry."

"We have five hours until the wedding," Eve said, taking the lid off the coffee and blowing on it.

David blew out a noisy sigh. "She's struggling, Eve. I think she wants very much to do the right thing for the baby—and for herself."

"Labor, especially one closing in on twenty hours, changes everything," Eve said. "For the last hour I was in there, she never looked at me. She didn't say a word, just powered through each contraction and closed her eyes. And no epidural, the little warrior. You know why? Because she thought it would be better for the baby."

"I can only imagine what she's going through," he said. "Having a baby and all the while not sure if she's keeping it or not. It's a lot for that girl. She's only twenty." David dropped back on his chair, looking as exhausted as she felt. "Any word from the family?"

"Angie and Noelle have everything under control," Eve told him. "Elizabeth is calm as can be. Noelle arranged for someone to come do their hair and makeup."

"You should be there."

"I'm not leaving, David. They're taking care of everything, watching the boys, promising to dress them and get them to the wedding. Noelle said she'd bring my dress and whatever I need to the hospital if this goes that long." And she knew it very well could. "I can't think about it now. What do you think Gabby's going to do?"

"I have no idea," he said honestly, taking her hand. "But whatever she decides, we will abide by that decision and move on with our plan." He leaned in closer.

"I like this hospital, where I would have much easier rounds, and Terrance and I have truly bonded over this. He's rooting for us, too."

She smiled. "I like him, and I think we'll be happy here. With or without—"

A woman hustled down the hall in front of them, and Eve instantly recognized her as Gabby's lead nurse.

"Let's go!" She leaped to her feet, spilling a little coffee on her hands but not caring.

They tore down the Labor & Delivery hall and stopped just as Gabby's door opened and Terrance walked out, scrubs, gloves, and mask on.

"It's go time," he said. "She's going to start pushing any second."

"Oh, oh." Eve sort of danced left and right to get by him, aching to get to the baby—no, no. To Gabby. The baby wasn't hers yet, but, oh, good heavens, she wanted it to be.

"I can't let you go in, Eve. Or you, David."

They both drew back, shocked.

"She's asked that you not be present for the birth."

Eve felt her whole body sink, almost like she wanted to collapse.

"Is there a problem?" David asked, going right into doctor mode.

"No, and I don't expect one. The baby's in the birth canal, exactly where she should be, and both mother and newborn vitals are excellent. But she just told me..." He swallowed and looked from one to the other, settling on Eve. "She's having second thoughts about the adoption and thinks it would be better to, uh, be alone when she meets her daughter."

Her daughter. Not Eve's. Of course.

Vaguely aware of David's comforting hand on her back, Eve nodded. "I understand," she managed to say. "We'll just...we'll be..." She gestured over her shoulder to the waiting room. "There. We'll be there."

With a nod, he turned and walked back into the room, the door open just long enough for Eve to hear Gabby cry out in pain.

And she did the same thing, only her cry was on the inside. Silent, heartbreaking, bone-deep disappointment that punched her in the gut.

"Come on, Evie." David wrapped a strong arm around her and led her to the waiting room, where an older couple waited, presumably for their grandchild.

Eve dropped into a chair and waited. Waited and waited and *waited* for something that wasn't going to be hers.

After a bit, she heard the other woman laugh, talking softly on the phone. After she hung up and whispered to her husband, Eve stared, guessing the woman to be in her late sixties. She had short silver hair and thumbed through a magazine, then looked off into the distance. She looked...like Mom. Or like Mom might look if she were alive.

Eve ached for her mother right then, a twenty-five-year-old pain grabbing hold of her with ferocity. It twisted and yanked and made her angry that she had to go through life without Jackie Chambers. Why wasn't she here to comfort and support her? Why did that truck cross the median and take her away? Would she have let Eve get this invested and this broken and this sad?

Why was life so dang *unfair*?

"Honey? Eve?"

She swiped at the tears soaking her cheeks and looked up at David, completely lost. But he was standing next to Terrance, who was smiling.

"She is born," David said softly.

"A healthy eight pounds, eight ounces, and twenty inches of baby girl," Terrance added.

"Oh." Eve shook off all the old grief and stood, prepared to endure a new one. "How's Gabby?"

"She did wonderfully. Long labor but short delivery. And she'd like to see you both," Terrance said. "Right this way."

Eve hesitated, not sure she wanted Gabby to see her this upset. David slowed at an end table, grabbed a few tissues from a box, and handed them to her before wrapping his arm right back around her.

"It'll be okay, Evie."

She nodded, dried her tears, and followed Terrance, who opened the door to let them in.

Gabby was propped up, her dark blond hair partially covering her face as she gazed at the bundle in a blanket she held.

"Hey," Eve whispered, holding back until Gabby looked up.

When she did, she gave a slow, unsteady smile. Oh, wow. This was gonna hurt.

"Come and see her," Gabby said.

They walked to the bed together, but David guided Eve closer to get the first look.

She tried hard to keep her gaze on Gabby, who looked beyond exhausted and a little shaky.

"It's okay, Eve," Gabby said, slightly lifting the baby. "She's perfect."

Eve finally looked down at the tiny face, the closed slit eyes, the button nose, and the most delightful rosebud lips already pursed and ready for a meal. She was pink and small and helpless and pure. Absolutely a miracle, like every baby.

"Oh," Eve whimpered, not trusting the tear ducts that threatened again. "She certainly is perfect."

"Ten fingers, ten toes, and she scored really high on that first test," Gabby said proudly.

"The Apgar," David said, leaning in. "She's obviously a genius."

Gabby chuckled at that, then stroked the sweet cheek under a pink knit cap the hospital provided.

"She's everything," Gabby said on a sigh. "I had no idea you could love another person this much, or this fast."

With every word, Eve's heart tumbled a little further, but she dug for composure and understanding.

"I know the feeling so well," she said. "And that love is real, Gabby. It's not hormones or childbirth or anything. It's real and it's beautiful, and I'm so very glad you feel it."

Gabby smiled up at her. "I do. I don't doubt that I love this child with every cell in my body."

Eve sighed. "Gabby, I—"

"Which is why I want her to have the best life possible."

Eve froze, staring at her while her heart nearly broke a rib, it hammered so hard in her chest.

"I want her...I want her...I want her to be your child, Eve and David."

"Oh!" Eve swayed at the words.

Behind her, she heard David let out a soft moan.

"She needs to grow up in your family, with the three greatest older brothers, and such a sweet mom and caring dad. She needs to live in that house and be rocked to sleep in that room and laugh and learn and grow and thrive."

Eve put both hands over her mouth, unable to stop the sobs.

Gabby's tears flowed, too, but she smiled through them. "And I need to grow up," she added. "I need to be in my twenties and go to college and know that she is always warm and safe and surrounded by love and aunts and...and...and you, Eve. *You.*"

"Oh, Gabby." She could barely utter the words.

"I don't know who taught you how to be a mother," Gabby whispered on a strangled sob. "But she did a really great job."

Eve almost collapsed, leaning on the hospital bed,

her whole body trembling. "Jackie," she managed to say.

"Your mom?" Gabby guessed.

"And what I'd like to name...our baby." Eve looked up at David, whose face was also wet with tears. "Jacqueline."

He nodded and came closer, taking a long look at the infant, and then Gabby. "Please don't say no," he said softly.

"To Jacqueline? I love it," Gabby said. "My grandma was obsessed with Jackie Kennedy, so she'd have loved it."

"I mean, don't say no to what I'm about to tell you," David clarified. "Eve and I have started a college fund."

"For her?" Gabby's face brightened. "See? I knew you'd take such good care of her."

"For you," he said. "So you won't have to work while you get your degree. And we planned to give it to you no matter what your decision was today."

She sucked in a breath, her jaw loose. "I don't...you didn't have to...I can't..." On a soft laugh, she closed her eyes. "Thank you. From the bottom of my heart, thank you."

Eve inched closer, her heart finally settling down but her arms aching to hold the baby.

"Here you go," Gabby whispered, lifting the bundle a little higher. "This is your daughter, Jacqueline...middle name?"

"Elizabeth," Eve whispered as she took the tiny

featherweight in her arms, fighting another sob. "Jacqueline Elizabeth Gallagher."

"I love it," Gabby said, falling back on the pillows in exhaustion. "I guess we'll have to do...legal stuff."

"We will," David said, beaming at his baby girl. "We'll handle everything and make it all official, whatever it takes. But now, does anyone care if I run through the streets screaming, 'I have a daughter!'?"

Gabby and Eve laughed, both of them still crying.

"And don't you have a wedding today?" Gabby asked.

"Tonight," Eve said. "We'll get there."

"Dr. R said she has to stay through tomorrow and I do, too. But then, you can take her home." She sighed. "And I guess I'll call NC State Admissions and see if I can start the winter semester."

Eve leaned over and kissed the baby's head, then did the same to Gabby. "Thank you."

Gabby held her gaze with a teary smile. "No, Eve. Thank *you*. I love you."

They held each other, staying until Gabby had to sleep and the nurses took the baby to the nursery.

On their way out, David and Eve stopped at the window for one last look at baby Jacqueline, who slept soundly in a clear bassinette on the end. As they stared at her with tears in their eyes, the older couple from the waiting room stepped up to the glass, beaming at a brand-new baby boy.

Eve turned and caught the woman's eye, realizing

now that she didn't look like Eve's mother at all, but the memory of those thoughts was crystal clear.

"Look at him." The woman tapped the glass. "That's Caleb."

"He's beautiful," Eve said.

She turned to Eve, her blue eyes bright with tears. "We're grandparents!"

"Congratulations," Eve said. "I bet you'll be the best ever."

The woman just nodded, too happy to even respond.

As they walked outside into the sunny December afternoon, Eve looked to the sky and sent love to heaven's newest grandparents, knowing they were watching, too.

Chapter Sixteen

Angie

HER HEART SHOULD NOT BE heavy today. Angie tried to focus on all the happiness around her, all the goodness in the air. A wedding day, New Year's Eve, being on the cusp of a new life despite some challenges were all reasons to celebrate. Everyone assured her that no matter what happened with the property—and no one had made a single move to pack or leave—they would figure it out.

Elizabeth believed in God's plan, and nothing was going to wreck her wedding day. Noelle had finally leaned into love and floated around the cabin like she was on air. Eve just texted from the hospital with the outstanding news that they had a new baby in the family. And Brooke, her darling, darling Brooke, had awakened and promised Angie that no matter what happened, they would stay in Asheville and start over together.

Where they lived was just a technicality, right? Angie should not feel blue today.

Sadly, she did.

She could barely stand to look around the two-story great room, knowing that these could be her last hours wrapped in knotty pine and the history of this home. Every time she closed her eyes, all she could see was what she imagined the ever-elusive deed looked like, with a state crest, raised letters, and signatures that would give them the legal power they so desperately needed.

Shaking off the blues, she was determined to join in the festivities, appreciating that they'd turned the cabin into a beehive of pre-wedding activity, and she should be part of that.

The hair and makeup crew that Noelle had hired set up tables and salon chairs right in the living room, with the fireplace crackling and the tall tree twinkling. They put on a playlist of "songs from the '70s and '80s" courtesy of Brooke, and popped champagne and OJ.

Aunt Elizabeth was downright giddy, flitting around in a white robe that said "Bride" on the back, her feet in slippers embroidered with "I" on one foot and "Do" on the other. For a woman who never gave two hoots about getting married, she sure was soaking up every joyous cliché about the whole process that she could.

The boys came in and out, mostly out of curiosity and still in the dark about the fact that they had a sister, which somehow added to the underlying vibration of excitement in the air. Eve and David wanted to tell them when they got home, so everyone kept the news quiet.

Cassie followed Noelle around like a shadow, fascinated by it all, asking repeatedly when it was her turn to sit in the "beauty shop" chairs.

"Angie, you're next!" The makeup person, Kelly, gestured to her chair. "And I can't wait to do a smoky eye on you."

"Not even sure what that is," Angie said, forcing a smile as she pushed up and headed to the chair.

"It's gorgeous," Brooke chimed in from her spot on the sofa, already stunning with her makeup finished, perfect down to the not-too-overdone false lashes. "And with your green eyes? Glorious, Mom."

Wrapped in a robe, Angie took her place in the makeup chair and gave in to the woman's hands on her face. "I'm all yours, Kelly. Make me glorious, as my daughter says."

"You already are," Kelly replied. "We're just going to accentuate what you have. And, my goodness, you and your daughter look alike. This is going to be fun!"

"Everything about today is fun." Elizabeth practically sang as she glided over to Angie's chair, a flute of what they all knew was ninety-nine percent orange juice in her hand. "I want you to be happy, my dearest darling."

"I am," Angie lied.

Elizabeth got right in her face, narrowing her not-yet-made-up eyes. "I know you too well."

"I am happy...for you," she finished. "I promise I'll rally. It's just that the clock is ticking and—"

"Pffft." Elizabeth flicked her hand. "Clock, schmock. We are under God's timing."

Out of love and respect, Angie didn't roll her eyes. But, seriously, all this talk of God's timing and clear paths had not produced a *deed*. God would be watching them move out and then He could supervise when Garrett bulldozed this beautiful home because... because *why*?

That might be the part that really irked her the most. Just to be sure there was no shred of a deed left, she supposed. Because if there was, and she hadn't found it, the—

"Mom, your phone's buzzing with a text," Brooke said.

"Anybody important?"

"Max Lynch."

"Oh." She leaned forward.

"You can't move mid-eyeliner," the makeup artist warned with a tap on her shoulder. "Texts can wait."

Not this one.

"Come here and read it to me, Brooke," Angie said.

She got up, tapping the phone. "He said, 'Hello, any luck with the deed?'"

"Bad luck," Angie muttered. "Ask him if maybe Attila the Hun is going to back off."

Brooke typed with lightning speed, then did a close examination of Angie's makeup. "Lookin' good, Mom."

"Thanks. Did he respond?"

"Not— Oh, yeah. He said he's with Garrett now, who is staying at the Inn at Biltmore Estate."

"Whoa." Kelly made an impressed face. "That place is pricey."

Angie rolled her freshly made-up eyes. "Why do I care where he's staying?"

"He says you have until six o'clock tonight, when Moneybags officially claims this property," Brooke said.

"We have until midnight!" she shot back.

"Mom, nothing's going to change between now and midnight. What should I tell him?"

"Tell him I'm going to our aunt's wedding tonight, and if he wants to rouse us and force us out of our beds with a forklift tomorrow morning, he's welcome to try."

Brooke typed, walking with the phone back to the sofa.

"Lashes?" the woman asked, dangling what looked like a small spider.

"I don't think—"

"Yes!" Brooke called. "Give her the works! And no crying once they're on."

She threw her hands up. "Sure. Lash me. I'm done crying."

In the other chair, Noelle was having her long dark hair French braided, with, of course, Cassie on her lap. "Ooh, I want lashes," Noelle said.

"Me, too!" Cassie sang out.

"Lashes? For you?" Noelle tipped the little girl's face toward her. "Yours are already perfectly long."

"I want to look just like you!"

"Ah," Kelly whispered in Angie's ear. "Your sister and her daughter are so cute!"

Angie just smiled, sliding a look to Noelle, who'd missed the comment, because she was deep in playful conversation with Cassie, as happy as anyone could remember. Surely Noelle would come to her senses soon and marry Jace. No career could match the joy that budding little family gave her sister.

And Eve would come dancing in any moment, mother of a new baby girl and planning her move to Hendersonville, basically down the road. Her delight would be palpable, and with good reason.

So everyone in the family was happy. Except Angie.

"Eve and David are here!" Elizabeth called as she peeked out the front window. "Should I call the boys down? Or maybe they want to tell them privately."

They all agreed to ask Eve and David first as Kelly finished pressing Angie's second lash in place. She stepped back to examine her work. "Let those rest and I'll finish with some setting powder. You go ahead and congratulate your sister. It sounds like there's a lot for this family to celebrate today."

"There is," Angie said, clinging to the words like a mantra. So much to celebrate. So much to—

"Hello, everyone!" Eve and David bounded in, both of them looking radiant, especially considering they hadn't slept since they'd torn out of here nearly twenty-four hours ago with a woman in labor. "We made the wedding!"

"Mom and Dad! You're home!" James led the pack of boys clumping down the stairs and headed for their parents, the decision about where and when to tell them now firmly in Eve and David's hands.

"Did that lady have her baby?" Bradley asked.

Sawyer ran in next, his teddy bear in one hand, a can of soda in the other. "Were you up all night?"

Eve laughed, giddy and light. "Yes, yes, and..." She frowned at the soda, then shook her head, letting the infraction go. "Yes, we were up all night and then some."

"Come here, boys." David stretched his arms out, beckoning his three sons closer. "Mom and I have some really exciting news to share."

"Did you buy that house in Hendersonville?" James asked. "'Cause we're fine with moving here."

Fortunately, they'd already discussed the move with the boys, who'd been uncertain at first, but must have been convinced. How would they feel about a brand-new baby sister—tomorrow?

"Bigger news than that," Eve said, giving David a nod that said they'd discussed this, and probably practiced it, in the car on the way home.

Around the room, everyone stopped what they were doing, and Brooke tapped her phone to turn down the music. Even Angie forgot her troubles as she realized she was about to witness a poignant and important touchstone in family history. The last that might ever happen inside these walls, so she decided to enjoy it.

David crouched down in front of the three them, one hand on James's shoulder, one hand on Sawyer's.

"Boys, you know we love you very much and we love this family."

Three faces stared back, completely uncertain how to respond to that.

"But sometimes families grow, and new children come in."

"Like you, Soy Sauce." James reached over and knuckled his youngest brother's head.

"And that's what's going to happen to us," David said.

James looked up at Eve. "You, too? Like that lady who was here for dinner?"

"Actually," Eve said, standing behind David with her hands on his shoulders, "that lady just had the baby girl that we're going to adopt as your sister."

"What?" James's jaw dropped. "A girl in the family? Oh, I don't know about this."

Bradley crossed his arms. "I think it's cool. Mom could use another girl around here."

Everyone laughed and looked at Sawyer, whose little hands squeezed the teddy bear he held, tighter and tighter, like he might...strangle the thing.

"You good with this, Sawyer?" Eve asked.

"Does this mean I'm not going to be the youngest anymore?" he asked.

"Yes," David said. "You'll have a baby sister and she'll need you to—"

"Hallelujah!" he screamed, throwing both hands in the air and letting go of that poor bear so it flew nearly to the ceiling and dropped hard and fast right over the makeup table.

Kelly managed a mid-air save of her cosmetics while Sawyer held up both fisted hands.

"I'm not the youngest!" he exclaimed. "I'm not the youngest anymore!"

The whole room erupted in laughter and cheers and hugs and happiness.

"What's her name?" James asked.

For a moment, Eve and David didn't answer, but looked at Angie and Noelle with wistful smiles, so Angie knew the answer before they said it.

"We're naming her Jacqueline Elizabeth Gallagher."

"Oh!" Elizabeth pressed her hands to her mouth. "That's beautiful! And she was born on my wedding day! Now if you all don't recognize that as a miracle, then I don't know what will convince you."

"That's a long name," Bradley said. "Do we call her Jack?"

"We call her Jay-jay!" Sawyer announced, still victory dancing around the room. "And I get to be the boss of her! 'Jay-jay, get me a toy.' 'Jay-jay, I need a cookie.' 'Jay-jay—'"

David laughed and shook his head. "You'll be a better big brother than that, Sawyer."

"I'll be the best!"

More laughter filled the room as Angie sank into her chair, giving in to the joy around her. There really was too much to celebrate right now. They'd figure it out. They'd live somewhere. They'd fight it in court. She had no idea what they'd do, but she refused to let the perfection of this moment be diminished by sadness.

"Let's get the setting powder on you," Kelly said softly, handing her the bear. "Can you hold this, please?"

"Now, let's get you boys in suits," David said, leading them off, then he sniffed. "Whoa. Showers first." As they walked up the stairs, David looked back at the ladies in the room. "I heard girls are easier. Guess I'm gonna find out!"

"Oh, Sawyer!" Angie lifted the bear. "You forgot your..." But he was up the stairs and out of earshot.

"Look down or close your eyes, Angie."

She cast her gaze to her lap, looking at the bear. It was truly old and beat up, most likely a toy that belonged to...Granny Jane? Maybe. It could have been her mother's or...

Suddenly, her whole body froze as she stared at the one lone button eye of the bear. The other was long gone, having left holes in the cloth, but...that button.

She'd seen that button before. Black, metal, with a curvy design and gold trim and—

"It was in the safe!" she exclaimed.

"Excuse me?" a few of them asked.

Angie pushed out of the chair, her makeup forgotten. "This button. That button. The one we found in the safe. It came from this bear!"

She looked around and saw a lot of blank and

confused faces, but not Brooke's. Her brown eyes lit up as she stood.

"Why would a toy be in the safe?" Brooke asked.

"Exactly!"

"What are you talking about?" Noelle asked, sliding out of her chair to come closer.

"The bear. This bear." Angie's hands were shaking as she flipped it over and found...a seam. "It's been re-sewn."

"It's old," Eve said. "I doubt it will last much longer the way Sawyer—"

"It might be in here!" Angie shrieked, her trembling hands plucking at the clumsy stitching. "The deed! It could be hidden here!"

"Open it, Mom!"

"Can I?" she asked Eve.

"Are you kidding? In the kitchen. Scissors!"

They all rushed there together, with Eve in the lead, snagging kitchen shears to give to Angie.

"I don't want to ruin the bear," she said, accepting them with shaking hands.

"Please! I just gave him a little sister to boss around! Cut!"

She snipped at the seam, which tore easily after the first cut. Was it possible? Could it be in here? Or was Angie just setting herself up for one more bone-deep disappointment and—

"Oh. Oh." She whimpered at the sight of something yellowed and old, rolled into a cylinder, embedded in the stuffing. "I think...I think..." Gingerly, she eased it out, her hands truly vibrating now. "Please don't be another recipe. Please don't be..."

Slowly, she unrolled it like a scroll, seeing the decorative black border and the official type and, finally, the words at the top.

Deed of Land

The screams around her—mostly Brooke's—were deafening but drowned out by one single thought and it sounded just like Sawyer: *Hallelujah!*

And the very top line showed the names she needed to see:

Mr. and Mrs. Garland Benson

The cabin was theirs!

They'd won. They'd *won*. They owned the property, and no one could take it away.

Angie started to cry, but remembered the lashes. Fanning herself with a hundred-year-old land deed, she just laughed instead.

"There's something on the back, Mom."

She turned it over, smoothing the curl to see some ink scratching. Lines and dots and an X. "What is this? It looks like a map of some kind."

Elizabeth leaned closer and peered at it. "If I had to guess, that's a sketch of this property. There's Creekside Road, the long driveway, and that X is where the house is."

"Let's get dressed, Brooke," Angie said, still shaking. "Ladies, we'll meet you at the church. We are going to make this official and then we are going to dance our booties off!"

"I SHOULD DO THIS MORE OFTEN," Angie said, strolling over the marble lobby floor at The Inn on Biltmore Estate.

"Visit super bougie hotels with the answer to your prayers, all dressed up to kill? Yeah, you should." Brooke laughed, looking more like twenty-six than sixteen with her professional makeup and blown-out hair.

"Yeah." Angie paused to catch her reflection in a large mirror, not even recognizing herself with the lashes and French braid. She'd donned her emerald-green cocktail dress that brought out the green in her eyes, and felt like, right now, she could do anything.

"The last time I was in a hotel lobby looking good, I dumped your dad."

"That was, like, a week ago," Brooke said.

"A lifetime. Any word from your boyfriend?"

Brooke snorted and shook her head. "He told his father we wanted to talk but I haven't heard back. What about Max?"

"He hasn't answered since I told him we were on our way over here."

"You should have told him you have the deed."

"I will, in person. If he doesn't come, I'll text a picture of it."

Just then, the giant glass front doors were swung

open by a bellman, and a tall man Angie instantly recognized walked in and looked around. It was a shame Max was the lawyer for her sworn enemy, Angie thought. He was a good-looking man, and in another life...

"Angie." He strode toward her. "Whoa. You look...nice."

"Victory will do that to a woman," she quipped, whipping out the deed and giving him a smug smile. "*My* victory."

With a look of surprise, he took the deed just as Brooke put her hand on Angie's arm. "Sam's coming down," she said. "Without his father, though. I'm going to talk to him."

"Okay. We won't be long. Will we, Counselor?"

Max looked up from the deed, the tiniest glimmer in his eyes. "Where was it?"

"You wouldn't believe me if I told you, but if you try and say that's not legit—"

"It is," he said, handing it back to her. "I'm happy for you."

"You are?" she scoffed. "Your client just lost."

"Actually, he's not my client anymore. We terminated a few hours ago."

She drew back. "He fired you?"

"No," he said with a laugh, the first real one she'd ever witnessed from him. It actually only made him better looking. "Other way around."

"Really? Why? You discovered you can't work for a heartless...you-know-what?"

"Not one who won't listen to my counsel," he replied.

"What did you tell him?"

"To drop this folly," he said, nodding toward the deed. "It made no sense to try and take the property from your family and, honestly? You'd win in court."

"And he wouldn't listen to reason? Why? The man is obviously loaded. Why would he even care about a cabin on the outskirts of Asheville?"

He searched her face, a hint of confusion and maybe amusement in his. "You really don't know, do you?"

"Know? What? About him? About...what?"

"Your cabin was built on a gold mine."

"Oh, I know that property is valuable, but he's worth..." Her voice faded as she stared at him. "Wait. What? Are you serious?"

"Yes. There's an unmined gold vein under your home that was discovered and logged in 1922."

Her jaw darn near hit the floor. "*Gold?* In North Carolina?"

"Absolutely. There's gold—well, there was—and gems and quartz all through the Blue Ridge Mountains, though most of it has been mined. But that vein? The one precisely where your house is? Let's just say if you bulldozed the cabin, you might find a nugget or...many more. Your home is sitting on hundreds of thousands of dollars, possibly more, Angie."

As he handed the deed back to her, she swayed a little. Then, very slowly, she turned it over, suddenly realizing the X was more than the location of the house, it was the location of the gold vein. "Did the Winchesters know this when they gave the property to my great-grandparents?"

"Louise knew," he said. "Garrett found her journal —one he had no idea he had until the Biltmore House contacted him—and it was all in there. She was the one who came from money and owned the land, but didn't want her husband to become a crazed gold miner. Without telling him about the gold, she gifted the land to the Bensons and required that they build the house exactly where they did—over the vein of gold. She thought mining was low-brow and didn't want to be associated with it."

"*That* was the stipulation!" she said. "I always wondered. But why wouldn't she want to tell them it was there? Or did she?"

"No one really knows for sure, but from what I've learned about this family, I suspect she didn't want anyone to have the gold. But you do. It's under your house."

No wonder Garrett wanted to level it.

"And there it will stay," she said softly.

His smile grew wider. "I had a feeling you'd say that. The home, the history—it's worth more than gold to you?"

"Absolutely." She exhaled, the truth finally making sense. "I don't care if it's worth millions, that cabin means more to me."

His handsome features softened into a smile of true

admiration. "Just one more thing to like about you, Angie."

"Mom?" Brooke came over, with Sam a few feet behind her. "Everything cool?"

Angie laughed. "Oh, you know me. LL Cool Angie."

Brooke rolled her eyes. "Can I ask you a question? Feel free to say no."

"I'm not going to say no to anything right now," she said, feeling giddy. "So ask big, honey."

"Not that big. I was wondering if Sam could come with me as my date to the wedding." She turned and included the boy in her conversation. "He doesn't have anything to do for New Year's Eve except hang with his dad and Sam just texted him about the deed, so he's—"

"Probably going to be in a very bad mood tonight," Angie joked, making them laugh. "Of course you can come, Sam. Bring your dancing shoes."

"Thanks!" Brooke shifted back to Sam, walking away as Angie turned to Max. "Well, there goes my date for the evening."

He lifted a brow. "I'm free."

"You're..." She laughed. "Serious?"

"Absolutely. There's nothing I hate more than a New Year's Eve alone."

He was serious and...it gave her a heady jolt of pleasure. She dipped back and took a good, long look at him, playfully giving him a once-over that didn't hurt at all. She'd never noticed how well built he was. But...

"Wait a second," she said, dragging out the words. "Are you...a gold digger?"

He threw his head back and laughed. "Not at all. I liked you from the minute I saw you, so if you say yes, I'll be your date and we can talk bad divorces and dance the night away."

She really didn't have to think about it that long. "You know, Max, I think that's a great idea. I'll text you the address and you bring young Sam Delacorte with you. Then I promise you the barn wedding of your dreams. Deal?"

She extended her hand for a shake, and he took it, but lifted it to his lips, planting the lightest kiss on her knuckles. "I'll be there."

Just as he released her hand, she heard a man call from behind her across the lobby.

"Hey! Angel! Messina! Chambers. Whatever you call yourself."

Without turning, she let her eyes shutter. "Now what does he want?"

"My guess? To make you an offer you can't refuse."

She snorted. "Watch me."

Very slowly, she turned and cocked her head, getting supreme pleasure from the slump in Garrett Delacorte's narrow shoulders and the downturned lips on his angular face as he loped toward her.

"Angie will do," she said, vaguely aware that Max had taken a step closer to her and that Brooke and Sam were a few feet away, watching.

"Angie." Garrett caught his breath, giving her the

joyous knowledge that he'd no doubt run down the hotel hall and banged on the elevator buttons, desperate to get to her. "Please. Can I...can I talk to you?"

"I'm late for a wedding, so no."

"Then I'll make it short and sweet. I'd like to buy the property. And I will make you an extremely generous offer, well above market." He rubbed his hands together nervously. "We can negotiate."

She moved one step closer and took the rolled-up cylinder of a deed and stuck it right under his nose, rooting for the perfect response. And then it came to her. What she'd told Brooke. What Eve and David learned this month. What all real families know and teach their young. What helped define and shape a person's happiness.

"Garrett," she said, leaning in, "there's more to life than money."

He just stared, defeat and disappointment in his eyes.

With that, she reached for Brooke and tugged her toward the door. As they walked away, she turned and saw Max Lynch smiling at her.

"Mom," Brooke sighed, sliding her arm into Angie's. "You're a rock star."

"Yeah. I kind of am."

Chapter Seventeen

Noelle

"WHAT GOD HAS JOINED TOGETHER, let no man put asunder," Pastor Daniel lifted an ancient family Bible, pressing it to his chest as he looked from the bride to the groom, his voice echoing through the church. "Jethro Dean McPherson and Elizabeth Maria Whitaker, I now pronounce you husband and wife. Sonny," he added, leaning closer to the groom, "you may kiss your bride."

As a cheer and applause rose, Noelle turned to Jace, eyes wide. "*Jethro?* His real name is Jethro?"

Jace chuckled. "Would you still love him if you'd known that?"

She gazed up to the front of the church, the joy between the newly married couple so palpable it seemed to come off them in waves. Cassie stood next to them, with Lucky resting on the church floor next to her. It was a picture Noelle would never forget.

"Yes, I'd still love him," she shouted over the noise, clapping. "Maybe even more."

Elizabeth—yes, Bitsy now—was radiant with love,

the beautiful and holy words of her marriage vows still fresh in Noelle's mind.

I promise to love, honor, cherish, and respect...until death parts us.

They'd hit Noelle in the gut, those words. The vow two people made up there was real and binding and forever, until death. What if death came sooner rather than later?

Well, it had for Jace. And still, here he was, on the very edge of doing it all again, if Noelle had the courage and strength to make that binding commitment.

I promise to love, honor, cherish, and respect...until death parts us.

The phrase danced in her head all through the closing moments of the ceremony, during the drive to the barn, and as they gathered under the fairy lights and white silk drapes to cheer the newlyweds when they arrived.

Noelle had been to a lot of weddings in her life— though never one in a literal barn—but none had ever affected her like this. None had ever made her seriously consider if she could or would do this.

Until this one.

After Elizabeth and Sonny danced to their first song—"Can't Help Falling In Love"—Elizabeth welcomed everyone with a teary speech. Sonny opened dinner with a moving prayer, and they ate from the glorious buffet. The air was nothing less than electric, all of the elation amplified by Eve and Angie's incredible news.

They were both going to live here, grow here, thrive here, and have days and nights of family time. And Noelle would be...in New York. For a while. Until she embraced change.

I promise to love, honor, cherish, and respect...until death parts us.

For a moment, Noelle looked around the barn, which had been transformed by light and love and a group effort that topped any big project she'd ever supervised. Everywhere she looked, she saw faces she'd come to know and love, and a few strangers who acted like family.

Everywhere was beauty and simplicity and heart and...goodness.

"You ready?" Jace stood next to her, holding out his hand. "The dinner's cleared. It's the family dance and David and Eve are already out there with Bitsy and Sonny. I suspect Angie's coming with Norm the New Guy. Join them?"

"Oh!" She stood, smoothing the maroon silk of her cocktail dress. "It's all going so fast. I feel like we just got here."

"That's how weddings go." He took her hand and walked her out to the center of the dance floor they'd rented for the event.

The strains of a song Noelle didn't recognize started playing as they stopped to hug and kiss the bride and groom, and do the same with Eve and David. Sonny's daughters, Caro and Hannah, joined them with Nate and Keith, and then Angie walked out with the rather handsome attorney who seemed as happy about the outcome of the property dispute as she did.

On a sigh, Noelle looked up at Jace and slid her hands over his shoulders to begin the dance, lost for a moment in his silvery-blue eyes.

"You good?" he asked, looking hard into hers.

"I'm great. Why?"

"You seem...distant."

"January looms," she said. "To be honest, I don't want this incredible month to end."

He pulled her in closer, letting their bodies touch. "Then don't leave."

"Jace, I...I have to. For now, anyway." She could hear Aunt Elizabeth's comment still, about her decision being "halfway" but that's how she had to do things.

"Who's that?" Jace inched to the left to look past her. "Definitely did not get the dress code memo."

Noelle turned and scanned the crowd to look...and her whole body turned to ice at the sight of the tall, thin woman in designer jeans, sky-high boots, a faux fur jacket, and a four-thousand-dollar handbag.

Her first thought was, *Did I used to look like that?*

Her second? "What the heck is Lucinda Butler doing here?"

"That's your boss?" Jace stilled. "Why?"

"I have no idea, but I think I'm about to find out." She eased out of his arms and looked up. "I've never meant this more, Jace. Pray for me."

He nodded as she turned and walked toward the

woman who could not look more out of place as she stood in the barn entrance.

Noelle lifted a hand to get Lucinda's attention, because she was looking around like poor sweet Doe a Deer in the proverbial headlights, her gaze landing on Lucky who'd sauntered over for a sniff of the stranger.

"Lucinda! What are you doing here?"

The other woman drew back, flipping her thick black blunt cut over her shoulders. "No, I think the question is what are *you* doing here? Honey, I get that you went country, but this? Is this what you call a hoedown?"

Noelle bit back her comment, remembering that Lucinda could be caustic, but she demanded respect.

"It's what we call a family wedding," she said. "And I think my question was appropriate. What are you doing here?"

"Is there somewhere we can talk?" She looked up at the hayloft, shuddering.

"Outside."

She glanced at Noelle's thin dress. "It's chilly."

"I'm fine." Noelle led her through the doors, down a snowy path dotted with red rose petals.

Taking Lucinda to the side between two Christmas trees, Noelle crossed her arms. "How did you even find me?"

"Your company phone has a tracker on it."

Distaste rolled through her. All this time, Lucinda knew where she was? She tamped down the response and just nodded. "And what could possibly be so important that you'd show up here in person on New Year's Eve? You could have fired me over email if you're not happy with the estate sale preparation."

And Noelle wouldn't have actually hated that, she realized with a jolt.

"Fire you?" She gave a soft hoot. "Honey, I'm here because I am the bearer of the best news ever and, frankly, you've been impossible to reach. I've called at least six times."

And Noelle had ignored every one. It was New Year's Eve, for heaven's sake, and her aunt's wedding. Lucinda knew that.

"I'm here to announce your promotion," Lucinda said, adding a smug smile.

"Oh, my..." In person? That was truly weird. "I thought that decision was going to be made in the middle of January, but that's lovely, Luc—"

"To the operations manager of Sotheby's London Luxury Art Division."

Noelle jerked back. "Excuse me?"

"You heard me," she said on a low laugh. "We've been crazy over there doing an international reorg, and it became apparent that I'm much more valuable in the C-suite in New York than running our division in London. And, Noelle, there was just no one else I'd consider for the job."

With each word, Noelle felt her whole body recoil more, backing into the tree so that the needles scraped her and the snow wet her dress.

"What?" she managed, which just made Lucinda laugh again.

"I knew you'd be thrilled! I know London has been on your bucket list forever, and honestly? It's cute and all, but not my cuppa." She laughed again. "See what I did there? Tea—you'd better get to liking it—is everywhere there. Now, I will go back with you, and we're booked to leave first thing in the morning."

No. No. *No!* She wanted to scream the word but, of course, nothing would come out. Because how could she turn this down? Running London was her lifelong dream! The reason she worked so hard and fought for every success and muscled her way past everyone and everything!

London was...it.

She managed a breath, but just got a mix of pine and Lucinda's cloying perfume.

Longing for an escape, she glanced into the barn in time to catch sight of Jace dancing with Cassie, twirling her in a circle, making her beautiful little face light up with pleasure and delight. Just past them, Angie was laughing with—what had he called the man? Norm the New Guy. They looked good together.

Eve and David were arm in arm, chatting with some of the guests, showing pictures of the new baby.

And...there was Bitsy. Yeah, *Bitsy*. With...Jethro. But her aunt was looking around, the first hint of concern on her face.

"Are you not excited?" Lucinda demanded. "Because this is massive, Noelle. And so's the raise."

More money. More work. More long days and lonely nights and an empty life with no goats, deer, kisses, or overalls. And talk about a long-distance romance! She might as well move to the moon.

For a split second, it felt like the Earth tilted, and falling off was a distinct possibility.

Trying to breathe, she held up a hand. "I...I need a minute, Lucinda. I'm...overwhelmed."

"Of course you are. That's one of the reasons I wanted to come." She put a hand on Noelle's arm. "I know this has been a rocky month for us, but I have truly come to appreciate your work ethic and I believe in you, Noelle. I believe you will knock this new job out of the park and then, who knows? The sky's the limit!"

Who knows? *She* knew. It would be another promotion, longer hours, more travel, and the occasional expensive handbag to reward herself.

"Please," Noelle said, stepping away. "I really have to think for a moment, Lucinda."

"About what?"

"About..." She caught another quick flash of Jace, lifting Cassie in the air. "What matters to me," she finished, walking away.

Her heels dug in the snow as she walked, making her unsteady, but she didn't care.

She'd just been handed everything...and didn't want it. Maybe the choice would seem obvious to an outsider, but London had been the most important thing in the world to her for so long.

Was it still?

"Noelle?" Elizabeth's voice broke through her thoughts.

"Bitsy? I'm over here." She stepped out of the shadows toward her aunt. "Don't ruin the hem of your dress in the snow."

She ignored the warning and came closer, arms outstretched. "I saw her," she whispered, pulling Noelle in for a hug. "You've either been canned or..."

Noelle leaned back. "Promoted to run the luxury art department at Sotheby's London."

Elizabeth gasped. "No! Not that I'm surprised, but...whoa. That's a major promotion. That's your dream. Congratu—"

Noelle stopped her by holding her hand up. "I don't know if I want it."

Elizabeth nodded. "Of course you don't."

"I mean, I've wanted it forever. But now there's Jace and family and you and...Jethro."

She snorted. "I knew that would throw everyone. I also can see that you, my dearest darling, are changing before my very eyes."

"Is it just because I want to be like you?"

"I'd love to be so prideful as to say yes, but..." She shook her head. "The hounds of heaven are after you, girl, and they are coming at you in the form of a flannel shirt-wearing sweetheart and his precious little girl."

Noelle searched her face, at a loss for how to answer that.

"A year ago," Elizabeth said softly, "I would have

told you to get on that plane and cross that ocean and live that dream."

"But...love?"

"But *God*. He has other plans. And I think you know what they are."

She bit her lip. "I love Jace. I love it here. I love... everything but what if I regret the decision? What if I wake up one morning and I think about London and I realize I walked away from my biggest and best opportunity? Or worse—what if something happens to Jace? People you love can die, you know, and—"

"And then you reunite with them in heaven. You cannot live your life with a bunch of what-ifs, and you know it."

She nodded, blowing into her hands as she realized they were freezing.

"Here," Elizabeth said, reaching into one of the beloved pockets to pull out a pair of white Chanel gloves. "You need these."

"Oh, I'm fine. They're yours."

She smiled. "You might need them for, you know, *something borrowed*."

Noelle choked a laugh. "Elizabeth!"

"You know I'm right."

"There they are!"

They turned to spot Angie and Eve working their way over the frozen ground to come closer.

"Bitsy, the caterers want to know if they can bring out the cake for cutting," Eve said. "It's out of the fridge but they're keeping it in the catering tent to stay cold.

We can bring it in anytime you're ready. Everything okay out here?"

Elizabeth and Noelle exchanged a look and a smile, silently knowing that somehow, in the last few minutes —and the last month—everything had become more than okay.

"Everything's perfect," Noelle said, a strange calmness settling over her. "We came out because..." She nodded to the woman hovering just outside the barn. "My boss paid an unexpected visit."

"Your boss is here?" Angie's voice rose in disbelief.

Noelle looked from one face to the other, her own dearest darlings, her sisters, her aunt, her family. "Not for long, unless she wants to stay for cake. Come on. I'll introduce you on our way to get the cake. She's over there."

She took her sisters' hands and Eve put an arm around Elizabeth as they walked to where Lucinda waited, hugging deep into her jacket, a scowl on her face.

"Lucinda, this is Angie and Eve, and we're the Chambers triplets. You know Bitsy McPherson, I believe."

"Bitsy Mc..." She shook her head and added a cool smile. "Cute. All of you, very cute. Now, when can we leave?"

Holding tight to her sisters' hands, Noelle locked her gaze on the other woman. "I'm not leaving, Lucinda. I'm not going to London or New York or anywhere. This is my home, this is my family, and that cute guy in there dancing with a little girl? They are my future. Would you like to stay for cake?"

Her sisters nearly broke her knuckles squeezing her hands, but Lucinda stared in shock. "Excuse me?"

"I'll come to New York in a few weeks and close everything up, but please consider this my verbal resignation."

Lucinda stammered a reaction, then just held up her hand to end the conversation, pivoted on her bootheels, and walked off. She was barely out of earshot when Angie and Eve practically flattened Noelle with questions and cheers and hugs and all the things she loved from her sisters.

Elizabeth just grinned and took it all in.

"I'll tell you everything," Noelle said. "But this is a wedding and I want cake!"

The four of them hustled down the side of the barn, still holding hands, laughing as they found their footing and came around to the back, when Elizabeth gasped and yanked them back.

"Stop!" she hissed.

They did, looking at her, then following her gaze to the edge of the tent tucked into the woods...where a black bear moseyed toward Caro's glorious creation, a two-tier red and white wedding cake covered in berries and mistletoe made of fondant.

"He's going to eat it!" Angie whispered.

"We need to scare him away," Noelle said.

"Uh, you guys..." Eve's voice wavered.

"It's okay, he—"

"*It's not okay!*" Eve started to move, but they held tight as they all spotted one very brave six-year-old boy on the other side of that cake, wide-eyed and terrified.

Noelle felt the blood drain at the sight of Sawyer facing off with the bear.

"*Do. Not. Move,*" Elizabeth ground out. "We can't scare that bear. He will...walk away."

But would he?

"Um, hey now, Mister Bear," Sawyer said, his voice shaky with fear. "That cake is not for you."

Shocking them all, Sawyer took a step forward, very gingerly lifting his hands toward the cake.

Eve gasped, but Elizabeth held her tight. "He's handling it," she said. "The bear's not scared of him, but he'll feel attacked by four of us."

Sawyer got his hand on the cake platter. "I know it looks really good and you would love it, but..."

The bear grunted and took one step closer.

"Oh, Sawyer," Eve whimpered.

"But you can't have it, big bear." He closed his little hands over the platter and used all his strength to lift it. "Go away now, buddy! Go! Shoo!"

The bear swayed a little, his focus on the cake, and none of them breathed.

Then he dropped his head, turned, and loped toward the woods and Sawyer darn near collapsed as he set the cake down.

"You are the hero of the night!" Eve hollered as they ran to Sawyer to hug his quivering, quaking little body.

"A bear warrior!"

"A cake-saver!"

He backed away, clearly stunned by his own bravery. "I faced down a bear," he whispered. "I did it! I finally did it!"

With a noisy cheer, they let one extremely proud little boy carry the cake in to an appreciative audience.

"This isn't the way home." Noelle peered through the windshield of Jace's truck through sleepy eyes that could barely stay open at two in the morning on New Year's Day.

"I just wanted to make a quick detour." He glanced in the rear-view mirror. "The flower girl is conked."

Turning to look at Cassie sound asleep in the back, Noelle smiled. "She was pretty excited when I told her I'm not leaving."

He reached for her hand. "At the risk of stating the obvious, that makes two of us."

Smiling, she let her eyes close, too tired to ask about the detour. For now, all that mattered was that she'd made the biggest and best decision of her life. She was staying in Asheville, living at the cabin with Angie and Brooke, and owning an art gallery.

More than all that, she would be in a loving and committed relationship with Jace, free to fall even more deeply in love—if that was possible.

When the truck stopped, she opened her eyes, but he'd turned off the engine and lights, so it was pitch black.

"Where are we?" she asked, sitting up straighter to peer into the blackness.

"Listen." He opened his door and she cocked an ear, hearing the trickle of Copper Creek.

"The fishing cottage? What are we doing here in the middle of the night?"

He just smiled at her. "Grab your coat and come with me."

"What about Cassie?"

"She's not moving and we're not going far."

Perplexed and intrigued, she tucked herself into the furry jacket she'd worn over her cocktail dress and stepped out onto snowy grass in heels for the second time that night.

Jace came around to her side to give her a hand. "Sorry about the inconvenience, but I wanted to bring you to a very specific place."

"Here," she said on a sigh, pointing to the side of the creek where a large flat rock had been their seat for fishing as kids, some kissing as teenagers. The very place where they'd last seen each other before she disappeared for twenty-five years.

He smiled and walked her a little closer, then turned her to face him, the sliver of moonlight providing just enough light for her to see the love in his eyes.

"Another Happy New Year kiss?" she asked, rising on her toes to get closer. "I'll take that."

He brushed her lips with his, then cupped her cheek. "I love you," he said softly.

The words warmed her against the chill. "I love you, too." She added a laugh. "Pretty sure I just proved that by turning down London."

"You're one hundred percent sure you won't wake up tomorrow and want to be on that plane?"

Wrapping her arms around his neck, she pulled him closer. "I want to wake up tomorrow and be in your arms. I will be...in my dreams."

"We could change that," he said with a sly smile.

"Oh, no. Not with Cassie. Not...no. I know it's old-fashioned, but I don't want her to come padding out to the kitchen some morning and find me pouring coffee wearing nothing but a flannel shirt."

He dropped his head back with a grunt. "Why do you have to put images like that in my head? I'll never sleep."

She kissed his chin, then nibbled a little. "Sleep is overrated."

Smiling, he tipped his head lower and kissed her, long and sweet and with so much love she could feel it in her frozen toes.

"So, Noelle," he said as the kiss broke and he held her tight. "Remember when we were here on that day twenty-five years ago?"

"Of course," she said, happy that the mention of the

day her parents died no longer caused any ache. "You asked me to be your girlfriend."

"And you never answered."

She laughed. "So you want to ask again and, this time, get yourself an answer?"

"I want to..." He took a step back, holding her gaze, his expression suddenly so very serious. "Ask you something else."

Before she could answer, he lowered himself to one knee, reached into his pocket, and lifted out a small black box.

For the second time, her world tilted. Her heart stopped and her whole body felt like it floated into air. "Jace..."

"Noelle Gloria Chambers, I am completely and totally in love with you."

She bit her lip, feeling the tears sting already.

"I never thought I'd find you again, or love like this again, or have this much hope in my heart, but I do. I've loved you since we were eleven, and I'm never going to stop loving you. Please, make me the happiest man on Earth and give my daughter the best present ever, and be my wife. Will you marry me, Noelle?"

With her hand over her mouth, she managed to nod as he flipped open the box to allow the moonlight to shine on the very engagement ring that had caught her eye the day they were in the jeweler's.

She could only think one thought, one line. One truth that once spoken would last a lifetime.

I promise to love, honor, cherish, and respect...until death parts us.

"Oh, Jace." She reached both hands out to him. "Yes! Yes, of course! Yes!"

She pulled him up to kiss her, spin her, hug her, and finally slide a ring on her finger.

Then he dropped his head back and hollered to the dark sky. "She said yes!"

"Shh!" Laughing, she squeezed him and kissed him again. "You're going to wake up Cassie."

"You bet we are. Right now." He started to pull her to the truck, then stopped, looking down at her. "I love you so much."

She laughed through happy tears. "I love you, too."

"Come on!" Holding hands, they made their way twenty feet to the truck, opening the back.

"Cass? Honey?" He put a hand on her shoulder and shook her lightly, unlatching the seatbelt of her booster seat. "You need to wake up, baby."

"Mmm. Daddy. Where's Miss Noelle?" she murmured sleepily.

"She's right here, baby. But you're not going to call her that much longer."

"Mmm." Frowning, she wiped her eyes and tried to blink, coming to consciousness to look from one to the other. "What? Why? What will I call her?"

"You can call me Mommy," Noelle whispered, her voice thick with emotion.

Cassie's eyes flashed, wide awake now.

"We're getting married," Jace told her. "Noelle and I are engaged."

"What?" She shot straight up and screamed the word. "Yes! Yes! *Yes!*"

She threw her little arms around Noelle's neck and gathered Jace in the hug, too. "You're going to be my mommy!"

Noelle squeezed them both and let the tears flow and the joy and magic of the mountain embrace her like her new family. She'd finally found her way home.

And *yes*...you can come back next year to catch up with the family and enjoy a whole new holiday adventure in the Blue Ridge Mountains!

The Asheville Christmas Tradition, book four in the Carolina Christmas series, is available to preorder now!

The Carolina Christmas Series

The Asheville Christmas Cabin – book 1
The Asheville Christmas Gift – book 2
The Asheville Christmas Wedding - book 3
The Asheville Christmas Tradition – book 4 (Coming next Christmas!)

But no need to wait to read more from Hope Holloway or Cecelia Scott. Individually, these authors have penned several bestselling women's fiction series that you can read right now. Both authors write about big, loving families living on the sun-washed beaches of Florida. The books are full of sweet romance, light drama, the occasional mystery, and lots of emotion. And they are all available in digital, paperback, audio and Kindle Unlimited!

Hope Holloway www.hopeholloway.com
The Coconut Key Series
The Shellseeker Beach Series
The Seven Sisters Series

Cecelia Scott www.ceceliascott.com
The Sweeney House Series

Hope Holloway is the author of charming, heartwarming women's fiction featuring unforgettable families and friends, and the emotional challenges they conquer. After more than twenty years in marketing, she launched a new career as an author of beach reads and feel-good fiction. A mother of two adult children, Hope and her husband of thirty years live in Florida. She spends her non-writing time walking the beach with her two rescue dogs, who beg her to include animals in every book.

Cecelia Scott is an author of light, bright women's fiction that explores family dynamics, heartfelt romance, and the emotional challenges that women face at all ages and stages of life. Her debut series, *Sweeney House*, is set on the shores of Cocoa Beach, where she lived for more than twenty years. Her books capture the salt, sand, and spectacular skies of the area and reflect her firm belief that life deserves a happy ending, with enough drama and surprises to keep it interesting. Cece currently resides in north Florida with her husband and beloved kitty.

Made in the USA
Middletown, DE
16 February 2025